W.W. JACOBS – THE SHORT STORIES
VOLUME 8

William Wymark Jacobs was born on September 8th, 1863 in the Wapping district of London, England. Jacobs grew up near the docks, where his father was a wharf manager. The docks and river side would be a constant theme of his writing in years to come.

Although surrounded by poverty, he received a formal education in London, first at a private prep school and later at the Birkbeck Literary and Scientific Institute.

His working life began with a less than exciting clerical position at the Post Office Savings Bank. Jacobs put his imagination to good use writing short stories, sketches and articles, many for the Post Office house publication "Blackfriars Magazine."

In 1896 Jacobs published Many Cargoes, a selection of sea-faring yarns, which established him as a popular writer with a knack for authentic dialogue and trick endings.

A year later he published a novelette, The Skipper's Wooing, and in 1898 another collection of short stories; Sea Urchins. These works painted vivid pictures of dockland and seafaring London full of colourful characters.

By 1899, Jacobs was able to quit the post office and write full-time.

He married the noted suffragist Agnes Eleanor Williams (who had been jailed for her protest activities) in 1900. They set up households both in Loughton, Essex and in central London.

The publication in 1902 of At Sunwich Port and Dialstone Lane, in 1904, cemented Jacobs' reputation as one of the leading British authors of the new century.

There followed a string of further successful publications, including Captain's All (1905), Night Watches (1914), The Castaways (1916), and Sea Whispers (1926).

Though Jacobs would create little in the way of new work after 1911, he still wrote and was recognized as a leading humorist, ranked alongside such writers as P. G. Wodehouse.

William Wymark Jacobs died in a North London nursing home in Hornsey Lane, Islington on September 1st, 1943.

Index of Contents
THE MONKEY'S PAW
MRS. BUNKER'S CHAPERON
THE NEST EGG
ODD MAN OUT
THE OLD MAN OF THE SEA
OUTSAILED
OVER THE SIDE
PAYING OFF
THE PERSECUTION OF BOB PRETTY

PETER'S PENCE
PICKLED HERRING
PRIVATE CLOTHES
PRIZE MONEY
THE RESURRECTION OF MR. WIGGETT
W.W. JACOBS – A SHORT BIOGRAPHY
W.W. JACOBS – A CONCISE BIBLIOGRAPHY

THE MONKEY'S PAW

I.

Without, the night was cold and wet, but in the small parlour of Laburnam Villa the blinds were drawn and the fire burned brightly. Father and son were at chess, the former, who possessed ideas about the game involving radical changes, putting his king into such sharp and unnecessary perils that it even provoked comment from the white-haired old lady knitting placidly by the fire.

"Hark at the wind," said Mr. White, who, having seen a fatal mistake after it was too late, was amiably desirous of preventing his son from seeing it.

"I'm listening," said the latter, grimly surveying the board as he stretched out his hand. "Check."

"I should hardly think that he'd come to-night," said his father, with his hand poised over the board.

"Mate," replied the son.

"That's the worst of living so far out," bawled Mr. White, with sudden and unlooked-for violence; "of all the beastly, slushy, out-of-the-way places to live in, this is the worst. Pathway's a bog, and the road's a torrent. I don't know what people are thinking about. I suppose because only two houses in the road are let, they think it doesn't matter."

"Never mind, dear," said his wife, soothingly; "perhaps you'll win the next one."

Mr. White looked up sharply, just in time to intercept a knowing glance between mother and son. The words died away on his lips, and he hid a guilty grin in his thin grey beard.

"There he is," said Herbert White, as the gate banged to loudly and heavy footsteps came toward the door.

The old man rose with hospitable haste, and opening the door, was heard condoling with the new arrival. The new arrival also condoled with himself, so that Mrs. White said, "Tut, tut!" and coughed gently as her husband entered the room, followed by a tall, burly man, beady of eye and rubicund of visage.

"Sergeant-Major Morris," he said, introducing him.

The sergeant-major shook hands, and taking the proffered seat by the fire, watched contentedly while his host got out whiskey and tumblers and stood a small copper kettle on the fire.

At the third glass his eyes got brighter, and he began to talk, the little family circle regarding with eager interest this visitor from distant parts, as he squared his broad shoulders in the chair and spoke of wild scenes and doughty deeds; of wars and plagues and strange peoples.

"Twenty-one years of it," said Mr. White, nodding at his wife and son. "When he went away he was a slip of a youth in the warehouse. Now look at him."

"He don't look to have taken much harm," said Mrs. White, politely.

"I'd like to go to India myself," said the old man, "just to look round a bit, you know."

"Better where you are," said the sergeant-major, shaking his head. He put down the empty glass, and sighing softly, shook it again.

"I should like to see those old temples and fakirs and jugglers," said the old man. "What was that you started telling me the other day about a monkey's paw or something, Morris?"

"Nothing," said the soldier, hastily. "Leastways nothing worth hearing."

"Monkey's paw?" said Mrs. White, curiously.

"Well, it's just a bit of what you might call magic, perhaps," said the sergeant-major, offhandedly.

His three listeners leaned forward eagerly. The visitor absent-mindedly put his empty glass to his lips and then set it down again. His host filled it for him.

"To look at," said the sergeant-major, fumbling in his pocket, "it's just an ordinary little paw, dried to a mummy."

He took something out of his pocket and proffered it. Mrs. White drew back with a grimace, but her son, taking it, examined it curiously.

"And what is there special about it?" inquired Mr. White as he took it from his son, and having examined it, placed it upon the table.

"It had a spell put on it by an old fakir," said the sergeant-major, "a very holy man. He wanted to show that fate ruled people's lives, and that those who interfered with it did so to their sorrow. He put a spell on it so that three separate men could each have three wishes from it."

His manner was so impressive that his hearers were conscious that their light laughter jarred somewhat.

"Well, why don't you have three, sir?" said Herbert White, cleverly.

The soldier regarded him in the way that middle age is wont to regard presumptuous youth. "I have," he said, quietly, and his blotchy face whitened.

"And did you really have the three wishes granted?" asked Mrs. White.

"I did," said the sergeant-major, and his glass tapped against his strong teeth.

"And has anybody else wished?" persisted the old lady.

"The first man had his three wishes. Yes," was the reply; "I don't know what the first two were, but the third was for death. That's how I got the paw."

His tones were so grave that a hush fell upon the group.

"If you've had your three wishes, it's no good to you now, then, Morris," said the old man at last. "What do you keep it for?"

The soldier shook his head. "Fancy, I suppose," he said, slowly. "I did have some idea of selling it, but I don't think I will. It has caused enough mischief already. Besides, people won't buy. They think it's a fairy tale; some of them, and those who do think anything of it want to try it first and pay me afterward."

"If you could have another three wishes," said the old man, eyeing him keenly, "would you have them?"

"I don't know," said the other. "I don't know."

He took the paw, and dangling it between his forefinger and thumb, suddenly threw it upon the fire. White, with a slight cry, stooped down and snatched it off.

"Better let it burn," said the soldier, solemnly.

"If you don't want it, Morris," said the other, "give it to me."

"I won't," said his friend, doggedly. "I threw it on the fire. If you keep it, don't blame me for what happens. Pitch it on the fire again like a sensible man."

The other shook his head and examined his new possession closely. "How do you do it?" he inquired.

"Hold it up in your right hand and wish aloud," said the sergeant-major, "but I warn you of the consequences."

"Sounds like the Arabian Nights," said Mrs. White, as she rose and began to set the supper. "Don't you think you might wish for four pairs of hands for me?"

Her husband drew the talisman from pocket, and then all three burst into laughter as the sergeant-major, with a look of alarm on his face, caught him by the arm.

"If you must wish," he said, gruffly, "wish for something sensible."

Mr. White dropped it back in his pocket, and placing chairs, motioned his friend to the table. In the business of supper the talisman was partly forgotten, and afterward the three sat listening in an enthralled fashion to a second instalment of the soldier's adventures in India.

"If the tale about the monkey's paw is not more truthful than those he has been telling us," said Herbert, as the door closed behind their guest, just in time for him to catch the last train, "we sha'nt make much out of it."

"Did you give him anything for it, father?" inquired Mrs. White, regarding her husband closely.

"A trifle," said he, colouring slightly. "He didn't want it, but I made him take it. And he pressed me again to throw it away."

"Likely," said Herbert, with pretended horror. "Why, we're going to be rich, and famous and happy. Wish to be an emperor, father, to begin with; then you can't be henpecked."

He darted round the table, pursued by the maligned Mrs. White armed with an antimacassar.

Mr. White took the paw from his pocket and eyed it dubiously. "I don't know what to wish for, and that's a fact," he said, slowly. "It seems to me I've got all I want."

"If you only cleared the house, you'd be quite happy, wouldn't you?" said Herbert, with his hand on his shoulder. "Well, wish for two hundred pounds, then; that 'll just do it."

His father, smiling shamefacedly at his own credulity, held up the talisman, as his son, with a solemn face, somewhat marred by a wink at his mother, sat down at the piano and struck a few impressive chords.

"I wish for two hundred pounds," said the old man distinctly.

A fine crash from the piano greeted the words, interrupted by a shuddering cry from the old man. His wife and son ran toward him.

"It moved," he cried, with a glance of disgust at the object as it lay on the floor.

"As I wished, it twisted in my hand like a snake."

"Well, I don't see the money," said his son as he picked it up and placed it on the table, "and I bet I never shall."

"It must have been your fancy, father," said his wife, regarding him anxiously.

He shook his head. "Never mind, though; there's no harm done, but it gave me a shock all the same."

They sat down by the fire again while the two men finished their pipes. Outside, the wind was higher than ever, and the old man started nervously at the sound of a door banging upstairs. A silence unusual and depressing settled upon all three, which lasted until the old couple rose to retire for the night.

"I expect you'll find the cash tied up in a big bag in the middle of your bed," said Herbert, as he bade them good-night, "and something horrible squatting up on top of the wardrobe watching you as you pocket your ill-gotten gains."

He sat alone in the darkness, gazing at the dying fire, and seeing faces in it. The last face was so horrible and so simian that he gazed at it in amazement. It got so vivid that, with a little uneasy laugh, he felt on the table for a glass containing a little water to throw over it. His hand grasped the monkey's paw, and with a little shiver he wiped his hand on his coat and went up to bed.

II

In the brightness of the wintry sun next morning as it streamed over the breakfast table he laughed at his fears. There was an air of prosaic wholesomeness about the room which it had lacked on the previous night, and the dirty, shrivelled little paw was pitched on the sideboard with a carelessness which betokened no great belief in its virtues.

"I suppose all old soldiers are the same," said Mrs. White. "The idea of our listening to such nonsense! How could wishes be granted in these days? And if they could, how could two hundred pounds hurt you, father?"

"Might drop on his head from the sky," said the frivolous Herbert.

"Morris said the things happened so naturally," said his father, "that you might if you so wished attribute it to coincidence."

"Well, don't break into the money before I come back," said Herbert as he rose from the table. "I'm afraid it'll turn you into a mean, avaricious man, and we shall have to disown you."

His mother laughed, and following him to the door, watched him down the road; and returning to the breakfast table, was very happy at the expense of her husband's credulity. All of which did not prevent her from scurrying to the door at the postman's knock, nor prevent her from referring somewhat shortly to retired sergeant-majors of bibulous habits when she found that the post brought a tailor's bill.

"Herbert will have some more of his funny remarks, I expect, when he comes home," she said, as they sat at dinner.

"I dare say," said Mr. White, pouring himself out some beer; "but for all that, the thing moved in my hand; that I'll swear to."

"You thought it did," said the old lady soothingly.

"I say it did," replied the other. "There was no thought about it; I had just—What's the matter?"

His wife made no reply. She was watching the mysterious movements of a man outside, who, peering in an undecided fashion at the house, appeared to be trying to make up his mind to enter. In mental connection with the two hundred pounds, she noticed that the stranger was well dressed, and wore a silk hat of glossy newness. Three times he paused at the gate, and then walked on again. The fourth time he stood with his hand upon it, and then with sudden resolution flung it open and walked up the path. Mrs. White at the same moment placed her hands behind her, and hurriedly unfastening the strings of her apron, put that useful article of apparel beneath the cushion of her chair.

She brought the stranger, who seemed ill at ease, into the room. He gazed at her furtively, and listened in a preoccupied fashion as the old lady apologized for the appearance of the room, and her husband's coat, a garment which he usually reserved for the garden. She then waited as patiently as her sex would permit, for him to broach his business, but he was at first strangely silent.

"I—was asked to call," he said at last, and stooped and picked a piece of cotton from his trousers. "I come from 'Maw and Meggins.'"

The old lady started. "Is anything the matter?" she asked, breathlessly. "Has anything happened to Herbert? What is it? What is it?"

Her husband interposed. "There, there, mother," he said, hastily. "Sit down, and don't jump to conclusions. You've not brought bad news, I'm sure, sir;" and he eyed the other wistfully.

"I'm sorry—" began the visitor.

"Is he hurt?" demanded the mother, wildly.

The visitor bowed in assent. "Badly hurt," he said, quietly, "but he is not in any pain."

"Oh, thank God!" said the old woman, clasping her hands. "Thank God for that! Thank—"

She broke off suddenly as the sinister meaning of the assurance dawned upon her and she saw the awful confirmation of her fears in the other's averted face. She caught her breath, and turning to her slower-witted husband, laid her trembling old hand upon his. There was a long silence.

"He was caught in the machinery," said the visitor at length in a low voice.

"Caught in the machinery," repeated Mr. White, in a dazed fashion, "yes."

He sat staring blankly out at the window, and taking his wife's hand between his own, pressed it as he had been wont to do in their old courting-days nearly forty years before.

"He was the only one left to us," he said, turning gently to the visitor. "It is hard."

The other coughed, and rising, walked slowly to the window. "The firm wished me to convey their sincere sympathy with you in your great loss," he said, without looking round. "I beg that you will understand I am only their servant and merely obeying orders."

There was no reply; the old woman's face was white, her eyes staring, and her breath inaudible; on the husband's face was a look such as his friend the sergeant might have carried into his first action.

"I was to say that 'Maw and Meggins' disclaim all responsibility," continued the other. "They admit no liability at all, but in consideration of your son's services, they wish to present you with a certain sum as compensation."

Mr. White dropped his wife's hand, and rising to his feet, gazed with a look of horror at his visitor. His dry lips shaped the words, "How much?"

"Two hundred pounds," was the answer.

Unconscious of his wife's shriek, the old man smiled faintly, put out his hands like a sightless man, and dropped, a senseless heap, to the floor.

III.

In the huge new cemetery, some two miles distant, the old people buried their dead, and came back to a house steeped in shadow and silence. It was all over so quickly that at first they could hardly realize it, and remained in a state of expectation as though of something else to happen—something else which was to lighten this load, too heavy for old hearts to bear.

But the days passed, and expectation gave place to resignation—the hopeless resignation of the old, sometimes miscalled, apathy. Sometimes they hardly exchanged a word, for now they had nothing to talk about, and their days were long to weariness.

It was about a week after that the old man, waking suddenly in the night, stretched out his hand and found himself alone. The room was in darkness, and the sound of subdued weeping came from the window. He raised himself in bed and listened.

"Come back," he said, tenderly. "You will be cold."

"It is colder for my son," said the old woman, and wept afresh.

The sound of her sobs died away on his ears. The bed was warm, and his eyes heavy with sleep. He dozed fitfully, and then slept until a sudden wild cry from his wife awoke him with a start.

"The paw!" she cried wildly. "The monkey's paw!"

He started up in alarm. "Where? Where is it? What's the matter?"

She came stumbling across the room toward him. "I want it," she said, quietly. "You've not destroyed it?"

"It's in the parlour, on the bracket," he replied, marvelling. "Why?"

She cried and laughed together, and bending over, kissed his cheek.

"I only just thought of it," she said, hysterically. "Why didn't I think of it before? Why didn't you think of it?"

"Think of what?" he questioned.

"The other two wishes," she replied, rapidly. "We've only had one."

"Was not that enough?" he demanded, fiercely.

"No," she cried, triumphantly; "we'll have one more. Go down and get it quickly, and wish our boy alive again."

The man sat up in bed and flung the bedclothes from his quaking limbs. "Good God, you are mad!" he cried, aghast.

"Get it," she panted; "get it quickly, and wish—Oh, my boy, my boy!"

Her husband struck a match and lit the candle. "Get back to bed," he said, unsteadily. "You don't know what you are saying."

"We had the first wish granted," said the old woman, feverishly; "why not the second?"

"A coincidence," stammered the old man.

"Go and get it and wish," cried his wife, quivering with excitement.

The old man turned and regarded her, and his voice shook. "He has been dead ten days, and besides he—I would not tell you else, but—I could only recognize him by his clothing. If he was too terrible for you to see then, how now?"

"Bring him back," cried the old woman, and dragged him toward the door. "Do you think I fear the child I have nursed?"

He went down in the darkness, and felt his way to the parlour, and then to the mantelpiece. The talisman was in its place, and a horrible fear that the unspoken wish might bring his mutilated son before him ere he could escape from the room seized upon him, and he caught his breath as he found that he had lost the direction of the door. His brow cold with sweat, he felt his way round the table, and groped along the wall until he found himself in the small passage with the unwholesome thing in his hand.

Even his wife's face seemed changed as he entered the room. It was white and expectant, and to his fears seemed to have an unnatural look upon it. He was afraid of her.

"Wish!" she cried, in a strong voice.

"It is foolish and wicked," he faltered.

"Wish!" repeated his wife.

He raised his hand. "I wish my son alive again."

The talisman fell to the floor, and he regarded it fearfully. Then he sank trembling into a chair as the old woman, with burning eyes, walked to the window and raised the blind.

He sat until he was chilled with the cold, glancing occasionally at the figure of the old woman peering through the window. The candle-end, which had burned below the rim of the china candlestick, was throwing pulsating shadows on the ceiling and walls, until, with a flicker larger than the rest, it expired. The old man, with an unspeakable sense of relief at the failure of the talisman, crept back to his bed, and a minute or two afterward the old woman came silently and apathetically beside him.

Neither spoke, but lay silently listening to the ticking of the clock. A stair creaked, and a squeaky mouse scurried noisily through the wall. The darkness was oppressive, and after lying for some time screwing up his courage, he took the box of matches, and striking one, went downstairs for a candle.

At the foot of the stairs the match went out, and he paused to strike another; and at the same moment a knock, so quiet and stealthy as to be scarcely audible, sounded on the front door.

The matches fell from his hand and spilled in the passage. He stood motionless, his breath suspended until the knock was repeated. Then he turned and fled swiftly back to his room, and closed the door behind him. A third knock sounded through the house.

"What's that?" cried the old woman, starting up.

"A rat," said the old man in shaking tones—"a rat. It passed me on the stairs."

His wife sat up in bed listening. A loud knock resounded through the house.

"It's Herbert!" she screamed. "It's Herbert!"

She ran to the door, but her husband was before her, and catching her by the arm, held her tightly.

"What are you going to do?" he whispered hoarsely.

"It's my boy; it's Herbert!" she cried, struggling mechanically. "I forgot it was two miles away. What are you holding me for? Let go. I must open the door."

"For God's sake don't let it in," cried the old man, trembling.

"You're afraid of your own son," she cried, struggling. "Let me go. I'm coming, Herbert; I'm coming."

There was another knock, and another. The old woman with a sudden wrench broke free and ran from the room. Her husband followed to the landing, and called after her appealingly as she hurried downstairs. He heard the chain rattle back and the bottom bolt drawn slowly and stiffly from the socket. Then the old woman's voice, strained and panting.

"The bolt," she cried, loudly. "Come down. I can't reach it."

But her husband was on his hands and knees groping wildly on the floor in search of the paw. If he could only find it before the thing outside got in. A perfect fusillade of knocks reverberated through the house, and he heard the scraping of a chair as his wife put it down in the passage against the door. He heard the creaking of the bolt as it came slowly back, and at the same moment he found the monkey's paw, and frantically breathed his third and last wish.

The knocking ceased suddenly, although the echoes of it were still in the house. He heard the chair drawn back, and the door opened. A cold wind rushed up the staircase, and a long loud wail of disappointment and misery from his wife gave him courage to run down to her side, and then to the gate beyond. The street lamp flickering opposite shone on a quiet and deserted road.

MRS. BUNKER'S CHAPERON

Matilda stood at the open door of a house attached to a wharf situated in that dreary district which bears the high-sounding name of "St. Katharine's."

Work was over for the day. A couple of unhorsed vans were pushed up the gangway by the side of the house, and the big gate was closed. The untidy office which occupied the ground-floor was deserted, except for a grey-bearded "housemaid" of sixty, who was sweeping it through with a broom, and indulging in a few sailorly oaths at the choking qualities of the dust he was raising.

The sound of advancing footsteps stopped at the gate, a small flap-door let in it flew open, and Matilda Bunker's open countenance took a pinkish hue, as a small man in jersey and blue coat, with a hard round hat exceeding high in the crown, stepped inside.

"Good evening, Mrs. Bunker, ma'am," said he, coming slowly up to her.

"Good evening, captain," said the lady, who was Mrs. only by virtue of her age and presence.

"Fresh breeze," said the man in the high round hat. "If this lasts we'll be in Ipswich in no time."

Mrs. Bunker assented.

"Beautiful the river is at present," continued the captain. "Everything growing splendid."

"In the river?" asked the mystified Mrs. Bunker.

"On the banks," said the captain; "the trees, by Sheppey, and all round there. Now, why don't you say the word, and come? There's a cabin like a new pin ready for you to sit in—for cleanness, I mean—and every accommodation you could require. Sleep like a humming-top you will, if you come."

"Humming-top?" queried Mrs. Bunker archly.

"Any top," said the captain. "Come, make up your mind. We shan't sail afore nine."

"It don't look right," said the lady, who was sorely tempted. "But the missus says I may go if I like, so I'll just go and get my box ready. I'll be down on the jetty at nine."

"Ay, ay," said the skipper, smiling, "me and Bill'll just have a snooze till then. So long."

"So long," said Matilda.

"So long," repeated the amorous skipper, and turning round to bestow another ardent glance upon the fair one at the door, crashed into the waggon.

The neighbouring clocks were just striking nine in a sort of yelping chorus to the heavy boom of Big Ben, which came floating down the river, as Mrs. Bunker and the night watchman, staggering under a load of luggage, slowly made their way on to the jetty. The barge, for such was the craft in question, was almost level with the planks, while the figures of two men darted to and fro in all the bustle of getting under way.

"Bill," said the watchman, addressing the mate, "bear a hand with this box, and be careful, it's got the wedding clothes inside."

The watchman was so particularly pleased with this little joke that in place of giving the box to Bill he put it down and sat on it, shaking convulsively with his hand over his mouth, while the blushing Matilda and the discomfited captain strove in vain to appear unconcerned.

The packages were rather a tight squeeze for the cabin, but they managed to get them in, and the skipper, with a threatening look at his mate, who was exchanging glances of exquisite humour with the watchman, gave his hand to Mrs. Bunker and helped her aboard.

"Welcome on the Sir Edmund Lyons, Mrs. Bunker," said he. "Bill, kick that dawg back."

"Stop!" said Mrs. Bunker hastily, "that's my chapperong."

"Your what?" said the skipper. "It's a dawg, Mrs. Bunker, an' I won't have no dawgs aboard my craft."

"Bill," said Mrs. Bunker, "fetch my box up again."

"Leastways," the captain hastened to add, "unless it's any friend of yours, Mrs. Bunker."

"It's chaperoning me," said Matilda; "it wouldn't be proper for a lady to go a v'y'ge with two men without somebody to look after her."

"That's right, Sam," said the watchman sententiously. "You ought to know that at your age."

"Why, we're looking after her," said the simple-minded captain. "Me an' Bill."

"Take care Bill don't cut you out," said the watchman in a hoarse whisper, distinctly audible to all. "He's younger nor what you are, Sam, an' the wimmen are just crazy arter young men. 'Sides which, he's a finer man altogether. An' you've had ONE wife a'ready, Sam."

"Cast off!" said the skipper impatiently. "Cast off! Stand by there, Bill!"

"Ay, ay!" said Bill, seizing a boat-hook, and the lines fell into the water with a splash as the barge was pushed out into the tide.

Mrs. Bunker experienced the usual trouble of landsmen aboard ship, and felt herself terribly in the way as the skipper divided his attentions between the tiller and helping Bill with the sail. Meantime the barge had bothered most of the traffic by laying across the river, and when the sail was hoisted had got under the lee of a huge warehouse and scarcely moved.

"We'll feel the breeze directly," said Captain Codd. "Then you'll see what she can do."

As he spoke, the barge began to slip through the water as a light breeze took her huge sail and carried her into the stream, where she fell into line with other craft who were just making a start.

At a pleasant pace, with wind and tide, the Sir Edmund Lyons proceeded on its way, her skipper cocking his eye aloft and along her decks to point out various beauties to his passenger which she might otherwise have overlooked. A comfortable supper was spread on the deck, and Mrs. Bunker began to think regretfully of the pleasure she had missed in taking up barge-sailing so late in life.

Greenwich, with its white-fronted hospital and background of trees, was passed. The air got sensibly cooler, and to Mrs. Bunker it seemed that the water was not only getting darker, but also lumpy, and she asked two or three times whether there was any danger.

The skipper laughed gaily, and diving down into the cabin fetched up a shawl, which he placed carefully round his fair companion's shoulders. His right hand grasped the tiller, his left stole softly and carefully round her waist.

"How enjoyable!" said Mrs. Bunker, referring to the evening.

"Glad you like it," said the skipper, who wasn't. "Oh, how pleasant to go sailing down the river of life like this, everything quiet and peaceful, just driftin'"

"Ahoy!" yelled the mate suddenly from the bows. "Who's steering? Starbud your hellum."

The skipper started guiltily, and put his helm to starboard as another barge came up suddenly from the opposite direction and almost grazed them. There were two men on board, and the skipper blushed for their fluency as reflecting upon the order in general.

It was some little time before they could settle down again after this, but ultimately they got back in their old position, and the infatuated Codd was just about to wax sentimental again, when he felt something behind him. He turned with a start as a portly retriever inserted his head under his left arm, and slowly but vigorously forced himself between them; then he sat on his haunches and panted, while the disconcerted Codd strove to realise the humour of the position.

"I think I shall go to bed now," said Mrs. Bunker, after the position had lasted long enough to be unendurable. "If anything happens, a collision or anything, don't be afraid to let me know."

The skipper promised, and, shaking hands, bade his passenger good-night. She descended, somewhat clumsily, it is true, into the little cabin, and the skipper, sitting by the helm, which he lazily manoeuvred as required, smoked his short clay and fell into a lover's reverie.

So he sat and smoked until the barge, which had, by the help of the breeze, been making its way against the tide, began to realise that that good friend had almost dropped, and at the same time bethought itself of a small anchor which hung over the bows ready for emergencies such as these.

"We must bring up, Bill," said the skipper.

"Ay, ay!" said Bill, sleepily raising himself from the hatchway. "Over she goes."

With no more ceremony than this he dropped the anchor; the sail, with two strong men hauling on to it, creaked and rustled its way close to the mast, and the Sir Edmund Lyons was ready for sleep.

"I can do with a nap," said Bill. "I'm dog-tired."

"So am I," said the other. "It'll be a tight fit down for'ard, but we couldn't ask a lady to sleep there."

Bill gave a non-committal grunt, and as the captain, after the manner of his kind, took a last look round before retiring, placed his hands on the hatch and lowered himself down. The next moment he came up with a wild yell, and, sitting on the deck, rolled up his trousers and fondled his leg.

"What's the matter?" inquired the skipper.

"That blessed dog's down there, that's all," said the injured Bill. "He's evidently mistook it for his kennel, and I don't wonder at it. I thought he'd been wonderful quiet."

"We must talk him over," said the skipper, advancing to the hatchway. "Poor dog! Poor old chap! Come along, then! Come along!" He patted his leg and whistled, and the dog, which wanted to get to sleep again, growled like a small thunderstorm.

"Come on, old fellow!" said the skipper enticingly. "Come along, come on, then!"

The dog came at last, and then the skipper, instead of staying to pat him, raced Bill up the ropes, while the brute, in execrable taste, paced up and down the deck daring them to come down. Coming to the conclusion, at last, that they were settled for the night, he returned to the forecastle and, after a warning bark or two, turned in again. Both men, after waiting a few minutes, cautiously regained the deck.

"You call him up again," said Bill, seizing a boat-hook, and holding it at the charge.

"Certainly not," said the other. "I won't have no blood spilt aboard my ship."

"Who's going to spill blood?" asked the Jesuitical Bill; "but if he likes to run hisself on to the boat-hook."

"Put it down," said the skipper sternly, and Bill sullenly obeyed.

"We'll have to snooze on deck," said Codd.

"And mind we don't snore," said the sarcastic Bill, "'cos the dog mightn't like it."

Without noticing this remark the captain stretched himself on the hatches, and Bill, after a few more grumbles, followed his example, and both men were soon asleep.

Day was breaking when they awoke and stretched their stiffened limbs, for the air was fresh, with a suspicion of moisture in it. Two or three small craft were, like themselves, riding at anchor, their decks wet and deserted; others were getting under way to take advantage of the tide, which had just turned.

"Up with the anchor," said the skipper, seizing a handspike and thrusting it into the windlass.

As the rusty chain came in, an ominous growling came from below, and Bill snatched his handspike out and raised it aloft. The skipper gazed meditatively at the shore, and the dog, as it came bounding up, gazed meditatively at the handspike. Then it yawned, an easy, unconcerned yawn, and commenced to pace the deck, and coming to the conclusion that the men were only engaged in necessary work, regarded their efforts with a lenient eye, and barked encouragingly as they hoisted the sail.

It was a beautiful morning. The miniature river waves broke against the blunt bows of the barge, and passed by her sides rippling musically. Over the flat Essex marshes a white mist was slowly dispersing before the rays of the sun, and the trees on the Kentish hills were black and drenched with moisture.

A little later smoke issued from the tiny cowl over the fo'c'sle and rolled in a little pungent cloud to the Kentish shore. Then a delicious odour of frying steak rose from below, and fell like healing balm upon the susceptible nostrils of the skipper as he stood at the helm.

"Is Mrs. Bunker getting up?" inquired the mate, as he emerged from the fo'c'sle and walked aft.

"I believe so," said the skipper. "There's movements below."

"'Cos the steak's ready and waiting," said the mate. "I've put it on a dish in front of the fire."

"Ay, ay!" said the skipper.

The mate lit his pipe and sat down on the hatchway, slowly smoking. He removed it a couple of minutes later, to stare in bewilderment at the unwonted behaviour of the dog, which came up to the captain and affectionately licked his hands.

"He's took quite a fancy to me," said the delighted man.

"Love me love my dog," quoted Bill waggishly, as he strolled forward again.

The skipper was fondly punching the dog, which was now on its back with its four legs in the air, when he heard a terrible cry from the fo'c'sle, and the mate came rushing wildly on deck.

"Where's that—dog?" he cried.

"Don't you talk like that aboard my ship. Where's your manners?" cried the skipper hotly.

"— the manners!" said the mate, with tears in his eyes. "Where's that dog's manners? He's eaten all that steak."

Before the other could reply, the scuttle over the cabin was drawn, and the radiant face of Mrs. Bunker appeared at the opening.

"I can smell breakfast," she said archly.

"No wonder, with that dog so close," said Bill grimly. Mrs. Bunker looked at the captain for an explanation.

"He's ate it," said that gentleman briefly. "A pound and a 'arf o' the best rump steak in Wapping."

"Never mind," said Mrs. Bunker sweetly, "cook some more. I can wait."

"Cook some more," said the skipper to the mate, who still lingered.

"I'll cook some bloaters. That's all we've got now," replied the mate sulkily.

"It's a lovely morning," said Mrs. Bunker, as the mate retired, "the air is so fresh. I expect that's what has made Rover so hungry. He isn't a greedy dog. Not at all."

"Very likely," said Codd, as the dog rose, and, after sniffing the air, gently wagged his tail and trotted forward. "Where' she off to now?"

"He can smell the bloaters, I expect," said Mrs. Bunker, laughing. "It's wonderful what intelligence he's got. Come here, Rover!"

"Bill!" cried the skipper warningly, as the dog continued on his way. "Look out! He's coming!"

"Call him off!" yelled the mate anxiously. "Call him off!"

Mrs. Bunker ran up, and, seizing her chaperon by the collar, hauled him away.

"It's the sea air," said she apologetically; "and he's been on short commons lately, because he's not been well. Keep still, Rover!"

"Keep still, Rover!" said the skipper, with an air of command.

Under this joint control the dog sat down, his tongue lolling out, and his eyes fixed on the fo'c'sle until the breakfast was spread. The appearance of the mate with a dish of steaming fish excited him again, and being chidden by his mistress, he sat down sulkily in the skipper's plate, until pushed off by its indignant owner.

"Soft roe, Bill?" inquired the skipper courteously, after he had served his passenger.

"That's not my plate," said the mate pointedly, as the skipper helped him.

"Oh! I wasn't noticing," said the other, reddening.

"I was, though," said the mate rudely. "I thought you'd do that. I was waiting for it. I'm not going to eat after animals, if you are."

The skipper coughed, and, after effecting the desired exchange, proceeded with his breakfast in sombre silence.

The barge was slipping at an easy pace through the water, the sun was bright, and the air cool, and everything pleasant and comfortable, until the chaperon, who had been repeatedly pushed away, broke through the charmed circle which surrounded the food and seized a fish. In the confusion which ensued he fell foul of the tea-kettle, and, dropping his prey, bit the skipper frantically, until driven off by his mistress.

"Naughty boy!" said she, giving him a few slight cuffs. "Has he hurt you? I must get a bandage for you."

"A little," said Codd, looking at his hand, which was bleeding profusely. "There's a little linen in the locker down below, if you wouldn't mind tearing it up for me."

Mrs. Bunker, giving the dog a final slap, went below, and the two men looked at each other and then at the dog, which was standing at the stern, barking insultingly at a passing steamer.

"It's about time she came over," said the mate, throwing a glance at the sail, then at the skipper, then at the dog.

"So it is," said the skipper, through his set teeth.

As he spoke he pushed the long tiller hastily from port to starboard, and the dog finished his bark in the water; the huge sail reeled for a moment, then swung violently over to the other side, and the barge was on a fresh tack, with the dog twenty yards astern. He was wise in his generation, and after one look at the barge, made for the distant shore.

"Murderers!" screamed a voice; "murderers! you've killed my dog."

"It was an accident; I didn't see him," stammered the skipper.

"Don't tell me," stormed the lady; "I saw it all through the skylight."

"We had to shift the helm to get out of the way of a schooner," said Codd.

"Where's the schooner?" demanded Mrs. Bunker; "where is it?"

The captain looked at the mate. "Where's the schooner?" said he.

"I b'leeve," said the mate, losing his head entirely at this question, "I b'leeve we must have run her down. I don't see her nowhere about."

Mrs. Bunker stamped her foot, and, with a terrible glance at the men, descended to the cabin. From this coign of vantage she obstinately refused to budge, and sat in angry seclusion until the vessel reached Ipswich late in the evening. Then she appeared on deck, dressed for walking, and, utterly ignoring the woebegone Codd, stepped ashore, and, obtaining a cab for her boxes, drove silently away.

An hour afterwards the mate went to his home, leaving the captain sitting on the lonely deck striving to realise the bitter fact that, so far as the end he had in view was concerned, he had seen the last of Mrs. Bunker and the small but happy home in which he had hoped to install her.

THE NEST EGG

"Artfulness," said the night-watch-man, smoking placidly, "is a gift; but it don't pay always. I've met some artful ones in my time—plenty of 'em; but I can't truthfully say as 'ow any of them was the better for meeting me."

He rose slowly from the packing-case on which he had been sitting and, stamping down the point of a rusty nail with his heel, resumed his seat, remarking that he had endured it for some time under the impression that it was only a splinter.

"I've surprised more than one in my time," he continued, slowly. "When I met one of these 'ere artful ones I used fust of all to pretend to be more stupid than wot I really am."

He stopped and stared fixedly.

"More stupid than I looked," he said. He stopped again.

"More stupid than wot they thought I looked," he said, speaking with marked deliberation. And I'd let 'em go on and on until I thought I had 'ad about enough, and then turn round on 'em. Nobody ever got the better o' me except my wife, and that was only before we was married. Two nights arterwards she found a fish-hook in my trouser-pocket, and arter that I could ha' left untold gold there—if I'd ha' had it. It spoilt wot some people call the honey-moon, but it paid in the long run."

One o' the worst things a man can do is to take up artfulness all of a sudden. I never knew it to answer yet, and I can tell you of a case that'll prove my words true.

It's some years ago now, and the chap it 'appened to was a young man, a shipmate o' mine, named Charlie Tagg. Very steady young chap he was, too steady for most of 'em. That's 'ow it was me and 'im got to be such pals.

He'd been saving up for years to get married, and all the advice we could give 'im didn't 'ave any effect. He saved up nearly every penny of 'is money and gave it to his gal to keep for 'im, and the time I'm speaking of she'd got seventy-two pounds of 'is and seventeen-and-six of 'er own to set up house-keeping with.

Then a thing happened that I've known to 'appen to sailormen afore. At Sydney 'e got silly on another gal, and started walking out with her, and afore he knew wot he was about he'd promised to marry 'er too.

Sydney and London being a long way from each other was in 'is favour, but the thing that troubled 'im was 'ow to get that seventy-two pounds out of Emma Cook, 'is London gal, so as he could marry the other with it. It worried 'im all the way home, and by the time we got into the London river 'is head was all in a maze with it. Emma Cook 'ad got it all saved up in the bank, to take a little shop with when they got spliced, and 'ow to get it he could not think.

He went straight off to Poplar, where she lived, as soon as the ship was berthed. He walked all the way so as to 'ave more time for thinking, but wot with bumping into two old gentlemen with bad tempers, and being nearly run over by a cabman with a white 'orse and red whiskers, he got to the house without 'aving thought of anything.

They was just finishing their tea as 'e got there, and they all seemed so pleased to see 'im that it made it worse than ever for 'im. Mrs. Cook, who 'ad pretty near finished, gave 'im her own cup to drink out of, and said that she 'ad dreamt of 'im the night afore last, and old Cook said that he 'ad got so good-looking 'e shouldn't 'ave known him.

"I should 'ave passed 'im in the street," he ses. "I never see such an alteration."

"They'll be a nice-looking couple," ses his wife, looking at a young chap, named George Smith, that 'ad been sitting next to Emma.

Charlie Tagg filled 'is mouth with bread and butter, and wondered 'ow he was to begin. He squeezed Emma's 'and just for the sake of keeping up appearances, and all the time 'e was thinking of the other gal waiting for 'im thousands o' miles away.

"You've come 'ome just in the nick o' time," ses old Cook; "if you'd done it o' purpose you couldn't 'ave arranged it better."

"Somebody's birthday?" ses Charlie, trying to smile.

Old Cook shook his 'ead. "Though mine is next Wednesday," he ses, "and thank you for thinking of it. No; you're just in time for the biggest bargain in the chandlery line that anybody ever 'ad a chance of. If you 'adn't ha' come back we should have 'ad to ha' done it without you."

"Eighty pounds," ses Mrs. Cook, smiling at Charlie. "With the money Emma's got saved and your wages this trip you'll 'ave plenty. You must come round arter tea and 'ave a look at it."

"Little place not arf a mile from 'ere," ses old Cook. "Properly worked up, the way Emma'll do it, it'll be a little fortune. I wish I'd had a chance like it in my young time."

He sat shaking his 'ead to think wot he'd lost, and Charlie Tagg sat staring at 'im and wondering wot he was to do.

"My idea is for Charlie to go for a few more v'y'ges arter they're married while Emma works up the business," ses Mrs. Cook; "she'll be all right with young Bill and Sarah Ann to 'elp her and keep 'er company while he's away."

"We'll see as she ain't lonely," ses George Smith, turning to Charlie.

Charlie Tagg gave a bit of a cough and said it wanted considering. He said it was no good doing things in a 'urry and then repenting of 'em all the rest of your life. And 'e said he'd been given to understand that chandlery wasn't wot it 'ad been, and some of the cleverest people 'e knew thought that it would be worse before it was better. By the time he'd finished they was all looking at 'im as though they couldn't believe their ears.

"You just step round and 'ave a look at the place," ses old Cook; "if that don't make you alter your tune, call me a sinner."

Charlie Tagg felt as though 'e could ha' called 'im a lot o' worse things than that, but he took up 'is hat and Mrs. Cook and Emma got their bonnets on and they went round.

"I don't think much of it for eighty pounds," ses Charlie, beginning his artfulness as they came near a big shop, with plate-glass and a double front.

"Eh?" ses old Cook, staring at 'im. "Why, that ain't the place. Why, you wouldn't get that for eight 'undred."

"Well, I don't think much of It," ses Charlie; "if it's worse than that I can't look at it—I can't, indeed."

"You ain't been drinking, Charlie?" ses old Cook, in a puzzled voice.

"Certainly not," ses Charlie.

He was pleased to see 'ow anxious they all looked, and when they did come to the shop 'e set up a laugh that old Cook said chilled the marrer in 'is bones. He stood looking in a 'elpless sort o' way at his wife and Emma, and then at last he ses, "There it is; and a fair bargain at the price."

"I s'pose you ain't been drinking?" ses Charlie.

"Wot's the matter with it?" ses Mrs. Cook flaring up.

"Come inside and look at it," ses Emma, taking 'old of his arm.

"Not me," ses Charlie, hanging back. "Why, I wouldn't take it at a gift."

He stood there on the kerbstone, and all they could do 'e wouldn't budge. He said it was a bad road and a little shop, and 'ad got a look about it he didn't like. They walked back 'ome like a funeral procession, and Emma 'ad to keep saying "*H's!*" in w'ispers to 'er mother all the way.

"I don't know wot Charlie does want, I'm sure," ses Mrs. Cook, taking off 'er bonnet as soon as she got indoors and pitching it on the chair he was just going to set down on.

"It's so awk'ard," ses old Cook, rubbing his 'ead. "Fact is, Charlie, we pretty near gave 'em to understand as we'd buy it."

"It's as good as settled," ses Mrs. Cook, trembling all over with temper.

"They won't settle till they get the money," ses Charlie. "You may make your mind easy about that."

"Emma's drawn it all out of the bank ready," ses old Cook, eager like.

Charlie felt 'ot and cold all over. "I'd better take care of it," he ses, in a trembling voice. "You might be robbed."

"So might you be," ses Mrs. Cook. "Don't you worry; it's in a safe place."

"Sailormen are always being robbed," ses George Smith, who 'ad been helping young Bill with 'is sums while they 'ad gone to look at the shop. "There's more sailormen robbed than all the rest put together."

"They won't rob Charlie," ses Mrs. Cook, pressing 'er lips together. "I'll take care o' that."

Charlie tried to laugh, but 'e made such a queer noise that young Bill made a large blot on 'is exercise-book, and old Cook, wot was lighting his pipe, burnt 'is fingers through not looking wot 'e was doing.

"You see," ses Charlie, "if I was robbed, which ain't at all likely, it 'ud only be me losing my own money; but if you was robbed of it you'd never forgive yourselves."

"I dessay I should get over it," ses Mrs. Cook, sniffing. "I'd 'ave a try, at all events."

Charlie started to laugh agin, and old Cook, who had struck another match, blew it out and waited till he'd finished.

"The whole truth is," ses Charlie, looking round, "I've got something better to do with the money. I've got a chance offered me that'll make me able to double it afore you know where you are."

"Not afore I know where I am," ses Mrs. Cook, with a laugh that was worse than Charlie's.

"The chance of a lifetime," ses Charlie, trying to keep 'is temper. "I can't tell you wot it is, because I've promised to keep it secret for a time. You'll be surprised when I do tell you."

"If I wait till then till I'm surprised," ses Mrs. Cook, "I shall 'ave to wait a long time. My advice to you is to take that shop and ha' done with it."

Charlie sat there arguing all the evening, but it was no good, and the idea o' them people sitting there and refusing to let 'im have his own money pretty near sent 'im crazy. It was all 'e could do to kiss Emma good-night, and 'e couldn't have 'elped slamming the front door if he'd been paid for it. The only comfort he 'ad got left was the Sydney gal's photygraph, and he took that out and looked at it under nearly every lamp-post he passed.

He went round the next night and 'ad an-other try to get 'is money, but it was no use; and all the good he done was to make Mrs. Cook in such a temper that she 'ad to go to bed before he 'ad arf finished. It was no good talking to old Cook and Emma, because they daren't do anything without 'er, and it was no good calling things up the stairs to her because she didn't answer. Three nights running Mrs. Cook went off to bed afore eight o'clock, for fear she should say something to 'im as she'd be sorry for arterwards; and for three nights Charlie made 'imself so disagreeable that Emma told 'im plain the sooner 'e went back to sea agin the better she should like it. The only one who seemed to enjoy it was George Smith, and 'e used to bring bits out o' newspapers and read to 'em, showing 'ow silly people was done out of their money.

On the fourth night Charlie dropped it and made 'imself so amiable that Mrs. Cook stayed up and made 'im a Welsh rare-bit for 'is supper, and made 'im drink two glasses o' beer instead o' one, while old Cook sat and drank three glasses o' water just out of temper, and to show that 'e didn't mind. When she started on the chandler's shop agin Charlie said he'd think it over, and when 'e went away Mrs. Cook called 'im her sailor-boy and wished 'im pleasant dreams.

But Charlie Tagg 'ad got better things to do than to dream, and 'e sat up in bed arf the night thinking out a new plan he'd thought of to get that money. When 'e did fall asleep at last 'e dreamt of taking a little farm in Australia and riding about on 'orseback with the Sydney gal watching his men at work.

In the morning he went and hunted up a shipmate of 'is, a young feller named Jack Bates. Jack was one o' these 'ere chaps, nobody's enemy but their own, as the saying is; a good-'arted, free-'anded chap as you could wish to see. Everybody liked 'im, and the ship's cat loved 'im. He'd ha' sold the shirt off 'is back to oblige a pal, and three times in one week he got 'is face scratched for trying to prevent 'usbands knocking their wives about.

Charlie Tagg went to 'im because he was the only man 'e could trust, and for over arf an hour he was telling Jack Bates all 'is troubles, and at last, as a great favour, he let 'im see the Sydney gal's photygraph, and told him that all that pore gal's future 'appiness depended upon 'im.

"I'll step round to-night and rob 'em of that seventy-two pounds," ses Jack; "it's your money, and you've a right to it."

Charlie shook his 'ead. "That wouldn't do," he ses; "besides, I don't know where they keep it. No; I've got a better plan than that. Come round to the Crooked Billet, so as we can talk it over in peace and quiet."

He stood Jack three or four arf-pints afore 'e told 'im his plan, and Jack was so pleased with it that he wanted to start at once, but Charlie persuaded 'im to wait.

"And don't you spare me, mind, out o' friendship," ses Charlie, "because the blacker you paint me the better I shall like it."

"You trust me, mate," ses Jack Bates; "if I don't get that seventy-two pounds for you, you may call me a Dutchman. Why, it's fair robbery, I call it, sticking to your money like that."

They spent the rest o' the day together, and when evening came Charlie went off to the Cooks'. Emma 'ad arf expected they was going to a theayter that night, but Charlie said he wasn't feeling the thing, and he sat there so quiet and miserable they didn't know wot to make of 'im.

"'Ave you got any trouble on your mind, Charlie," ses Mrs. Cook, "or is it the tooth-ache?"

"It ain't the toothache," ses Charlie.

He sat there pulling a long face and staring at the floor, but all Mrs. Cook and Emma could do 'e wouldn't tell them wot was the matter with 'im. He said 'e didn't want to worry other people with 'is troubles; let everybody bear their own, that was 'is motto. Even when George Smith offered to go to the theayter with Emma instead of 'im he didn't fire up, and, if it 'adn't ha' been for Mrs. Cook, George wouldn't ha' been sorry that 'e spoke.

"Theayters ain't for me," ses Charlie, with a groan. "I'm more likely to go to gaol, so far as I can see, than a theayter."

Mrs. Cook and Emma both screamed and Sarah Ann did 'er first highstericks, and very well, too, considering that she 'ad only just turned fifteen.

"Gaol!" ses old Cook, as soon as they 'ad quieted Sarah Ann with a bowl o' cold water that young Bill 'ad the presence o' mind to go and fetch. "Gaol! What for?"

"You wouldn't believe if I was to tell you." ses Charlie, getting up to go, "and besides, I don't want any of you to think as 'ow I am worse than wot I am."

He shook his 'cad at them sorrowful-like, and afore they could stop 'im he 'ad gone. Old Cook shouted arter 'im, but it was no use, and the others was running into the scullery to fill the bowl agin for Emma.

Mrs. Cook went round to 'is lodgings next morning, but found that 'e was out. They began to fancy all sorts o' things then, but Charlie turned up agin that evening more miserable than ever.

"I went round to see you this morning," ses Mrs. Cook, "but you wasn't at 'ome."

"I never am, 'ardly," ses Charlie. "I can't be—it ain't safe."

"Why not?" ses Mrs. Cook, fidgeting.

"If I was to tell you, you'd lose your good opinion of me," ses Charlie.

"It wouldn't be much to lose," ses Mrs. Cook, firing up.

Charlie didn't answer 'er. When he did speak he spoke to the old man, and he was so down-'arted that 'e gave 'im the chills a'most, He 'ardly took any notice of Emma, and, when Mrs. Cook spoke about the shop again, said that chandlers' shops was for happy people, not for 'im.

By the time they sat down to supper they was nearly all as miserable as Charlie 'imself. From words he let drop they all seemed to 'ave the idea that the police was arter 'im, and Mrs. Cook was just asking 'im for wot she called the third and last time, but wot was more likely the hundred and third, wot he'd done, when there was a knock at the front door, so loud and so sudden that old Cook and young Bill both cut their mouths at the same time.

"Anybody 'ere o' the name of Emma Cook?" ses a man's voice, when young Bill opened the door.

"She's inside," ses the boy, and the next moment Jack Bates followed 'im into the room, and then fell back with a start as 'e saw Charlie Tagg.

"Ho, 'ere you are, are you?" he ses, looking at 'im very black. "Wot's the matter?" ses Mrs. Cook, very sharp.

"I didn't expect to 'ave the pleasure o' seeing you 'ere, my lad," ses Jack, still staring at Charlie, and twisting 'is face up into awful scowls. "Which is Emma Cook?"

"Miss Cook is my name," ses Emma, very sharp. "Wot d'ye want?"

"Very good," ses Jack Bates, looking at Charlie agin; "then p'r'aps you'll do me the kindness of telling that lie o' yours agin afore this young lady."

"It's the truth," ses Charlie, looking down at 'is plate.

"If somebody don't tell me wot all this is about in two minutes, I shall do something desprit," ses Mrs. Cook, getting up.

"This 'ere—er—man," ses Jack Bates, pointing at Charlie, "owes me seventy-five pounds and won't pay. When I ask 'im for it he ses a party he's keeping company with, by the name of Emma Cook, 'as got it, and he can't get it."

"So she has," ses Charlie, without looking up.

"Wot does 'e owe you the money for?" ses Mrs. Cook.

"'Cos I lent it to 'im," ses Jack.

"Lent it? What for?" ses Mrs. Cook.

"'Cos I was a fool, I s'pose," ses jack Bates; "a good-natured fool. Anyway, I'm sick and tired of asking for it, and if I don't get it to-night I'm going to see the police about it."

He sat down on a chair with 'is hat cocked over one eye, and they all sat staring at 'im as though they didn't know wot to say next.

"So this is wot you meant when you said you'd got the chance of a lifetime, is it?" ses Mrs. Cook to Charlie. "This is wot you wanted it for, is it? Wot did you borrow all that money for?"

"Spend," ses Charlie, in a sulky voice.

"Spend!" ses Mrs. Cook, with a scream; "wot in?"

"Drink and cards mostly," ses Jack Bates, remembering wot Charlie 'ad told 'im about blackening 'is character.

You might ha' heard a pin drop a'most, and Charlie sat there without saying a word.

"Charlie's been led away," ses Mrs. Cook, looking 'ard at Jack Bates. "I s'pose you lent 'im the money to win it back from 'im at cards, didn't you?"

"And gave 'im too much licker fust," ses old Cook. "I've 'eard of your kind. If Charlie takes my advice 'e won't pay you a farthing. I should let you do your worst if I was 'im; that's wot I should do. You've got a low face; a nasty, ugly, low face."

"One o' the worst I ever see," ses Mrs. Cook. "It looks as though it might ha' been cut out o' the Police News."

"'Owever could you ha' trusted a man with a face like that, Charlie?" ses old Cook. "Come away from 'im, Bill; I don't like such a chap in the room."

Jack Bates began to feel very awk'ard. They was all glaring at 'im as though they could eat 'im, and he wasn't used to such treatment. And, as a matter o' fact, he'd got a very good-'arted face.

"You go out o' that door," ses old Cook, pointing to it. "Go and do your worst. You won't get any money 'ere."

"Stop a minute," ses Emma, and afore they could stop 'er she ran upstairs. Mrs. Cook went arter 'er and 'igh words was heard up in the bedroom, but by-and-by Emma came down holding her head very 'igh and looking at Jack Bates as though he was dirt.

"How am I to know Charlie owes you this money?" she ses.

Jack Bates turned very red, and arter fumbling in 'is pockets took out about a dozen dirty bits o' paper, which Charlie 'ad given 'im for I O U's. Emma read 'em all, and then she threw a little parcel on the table.

"There's your money," she ses; "take it and go."

Mrs. Cook and 'er father began to call out, but it was no good.

"There's seventy-two pounds there," ses Emma, who was very pale; "and 'ere's a ring you can have to 'elp make up the rest." And she drew Charlie's ring off and throwed it on the table. "I've done with 'im for good," she ses, with a look at 'er mother.

Jack Bates took up the money and the ring and stood there looking at 'er and trying to think wot to say. He'd always been uncommon partial to the sex, and it did seem 'ard to stand there and take all that on account of Charlie Tagg.

"I only wanted my own," he ses, at last, shuffling about the floor.

"Well, you've got it," ses Mrs. Cook, "and now you can go."

"You're pi'soning the air of my front parlour," ses old Cook, opening the winder a little at the top.

"P'r'aps I ain't so bad as you think I am," ses Jack Bates, still looking at Emma, and with that 'e walked over to Charlie and dumped down the money on the table in front of 'im. "Take it," he ses, "and don't borrow any more. I make you a free gift of it. P'r'aps my 'art ain't as black as my face," he ses, turning to Mrs. Cook.

They was all so surprised at fust that they couldn't speak, but old Cook smiled at 'im and put the winder up agin. And Charlie Tagg sat there arf mad with temper, locking as though 'e could eat Jack Bates without any salt, as the saying is.

"I—I can't take it," he ses at last, with a stammer.

"Can't take it? Why not?" ses old Cook, staring. "This gentleman 'as given it to you." "A free gift," ses Mrs. Cook, smiling at Jack very sweet.

"I can't take it," ses Charlie, winking at Jack to take the money up and give it to 'im quiet, as arranged. "I 'ave my pride."

"So 'ave I," ses Jack. "Are you going to take it?"

Charlie gave another look. "No," he ses, "I cant take a favour. I borrowed the money and I'll pay it back.

"Very good," ses Jack, taking it up. "It's my money, ain't it?"

"Yes," ses Charlie, taking no notice of Mrs. Cook and 'er husband, wot was both talking to 'im at once, and trying to persuade 'im to alter his mind.

"Then I give it to Miss Emma Cook," ses Jack Bates, putting it into her hands. "Good-night everybody and good luck."

He slammed the front door behind 'im and they 'eard 'im go off down the road as if 'e was going for fire-engines. Charlie sat there for a moment struck all of a heap, and then 'e jumped up and dashed arter 'im. He just saw 'im disappearing round a corner, and he didn't see 'im agin for a couple o' year arterwards, by which time the Sydney gal had 'ad three or four young men arter 'im, and Emma, who 'ad changed her name to Smith, was doing one o' the best businesses in the chandlery line in Poplar.

ODD MAN OUT

The night watchman pursed up his lips and shook his head. Friendship, he said, decidedly, is a deloosion and a snare. I've 'ad more friendships in my life than most people—owing to being took a fancy to for some reason or other—and they nearly all came to a sudden ending.

I remember one man who used to think I couldn't do wrong; everything I did was right to 'im; and now if I pass 'im in the street he makes a face as if he'd got a hair in 'is mouth. All because I told 'im the truth one day when he was thinking of getting married. Being a bit uneasy-like in his mind, he asked me 'ow, supposing I was a gal, his looks would strike me.

It was an orkard question, and I told him that he 'ad got a good 'art and that no man could 'ave a better pal. I said he 'ad got a good temper and was free with 'is money. O' course, that didn't satisfy 'im, and at last he told me to take a good look at 'im and tell him wot I thought of 'is looks. There was no getting out of it, and at last I 'ad to tell him plain that everybody 'ad diff'rent ideas about looks; that looks wasn't everything; and that 'andsome is as 'andsome does. Even then 'e wasn't satisfied, and at last I told 'im, speaking as a pal to a pal, that if I was a gal and he came along trying to court me, I should go to the police about it.

I remember two young fellers that was shipmates with me some years ago, and they was such out-and-out pals that everybody called 'em the Siamese twins. They always shipped together and shared lodgings together when they was ashore, and Ted Denver would no more 'ave thought of going out without Charlie Brice than Charlie Brice would 'ave thought of going out without 'im. They shared their baccy and their money and everything else, and it's my opinion that if they 'ad only 'ad one pair o' boots between 'em they'd 'ave hopped along in one each.

They 'ad been like it for years, and they kept it up when they left the sea and got berths ashore. Anybody knowing them would ha' thought that nothing but death could part 'em; but it happened otherwise.

There was a gal in it, of course. A gal that Ted Denver got into conversation with on top of a bus, owing to her steadying 'erself by putting her hand on 'is shoulder as she passed 'im. Bright, lively sort o' gal she seemed, and, afore Ted knew where he was, they was talking away as though they 'ad known each other for years.

Charlie didn't seem to care much for it at fust, but he didn't raise no objection; and when the gal got up to go he stopped the bus for 'er by poking the driver in the back, and they all got off together. Ted went fust to break her fall, in case the bus started off too sudden, and Charlie 'elped her down behind by catching hold of a lace collar she was wearing. When she turned to speak to 'im about it, she knocked the conductor's hat off with 'er umbrella, and there was so much unpleasantness that by the time they 'ad got to the pavement she told Charlie that she never wanted to see his silly fat face agin.

"It ain't fat," ses Ted, speaking up for 'im; "it's the shape of it."

"And it ain't silly," ses Charlie, speaking very quick; "mind that!"

"It's a bit o' real lace," ses the gal, twisting her 'ead round to look at the collar; "it cost me one and two-three only last night."

"One an' *wot?*" ses Charlie, who, not being a married man, didn't understand 'er.

"One shilling," ses the gal, "two pennies, and three farthings. D'ye understand that?"

"Yes," ses Charlie.

"He's cleverer than he looks," ses the gal, turning to Ted. "I s'pose you're right, and it is the shape after all."

Ted walked along one side of 'er and Charlie the other, till they came to the corner of the road where she lived, and then Ted and 'er stood there talking till Charlie got sick and tired of it, and kept tugging at Ted's coat for 'im to come away.

"I'm coming," ses Ted, at last. "I s'pose you won't be this way to-morrow night?" he ses, turning to the gal.

"I might if I thought there was no chance of seeing you," she ses, tossing her 'ead.

"You needn't be alarmed," ses Charlie, shoving in his oar; "we're going to a music-'all to-morrow night."

"Oh, go to your blessed music-'all," ses the gal to Ted; "I don't want you."

She turned round and a'most ran up the road, with Ted follering 'er and begging of 'er not to be so hasty, and afore they parted she told 'im that 'er name was. Emma White, and promised to meet 'im there the next night at seven.

O' course Mr. Charlie Brice turned up alongside o' Ted the next night, and at fust Emma said she was going straight off 'ome agin. She did go part o' the way, and then, when she found that Ted wouldn't send his mate off, she came back and, woman-like, said as 'ow she wasn't going to go 'ome just to please Charlie Brice. She wouldn't speak a word to 'im, and when they all went to the music-'all together she sat with her face turned away from 'im and her elbow sticking in 'is chest. Doing that and watching the performance at the same time gave 'er a stiff neck, and she got in such a temper over it she wouldn't hardly speak to Ted, and when Charlie—meaning well—told 'er to rub it with a bit o' mutton-fat she nearly went off her 'ead.

"Who asked you to come with us?" she ses, as soon as she could speak. "'Ow dare you force yourself where you ain't wanted?"

"Ted wants me," ses Charlie.

"We've been together for years," ses Ted. "You'll like Charlie when you get used to 'im—everybody does."

"Not me!" ses Emma, with a shiver. "It gives me the fair creeps to look at him. You'll 'ave to choose between us. If he comes, I sha'n't. Which is it to be?"

Neither of 'em answered 'er, but the next night they both turned up as usual, and Emma White stood there looking at 'em and nearly crying with temper.

"'Ow would you like it if I brought another young lady with me?" she ses to Ted.

"It wouldn't make no difference to me," ses Ted. "Any friend o' yours is welcome."

Emma stood looking at 'em, and then she patted 'er eyes with a pocket-'ankercher and began to look more cheerful.

"You ain't the only one that has got a dear friend," she says, looking. at 'im and wiping 'er lips with the 'ankercher. "I've got one, and if Charlie Brice don't promise to stay at 'ome to-morrow night I'll bring her with me."

"Bring 'er, and welcome," ses Ted.

"I sha'n't stay at 'ome for fifty dear friends," ses Charlie.

"Have it your own way," ses Emma. "If you come, Sophy Jennings comes, that's all."

She was as good as 'er word, too, and next night when they turned up they found Emma and 'er friend waiting for them. Charlie thought it was the friend's mother at fust, but he found out arterwards that she was a widder-woman. She had 'ad two husbands, and both of 'em 'ad passed away with a smile on their face. She seemed to take a fancy to Charlie the moment she set eyes on 'im, and two or three times, they'd 'ave lost Ted and Emma if it hadn't been for 'im.

They did lose 'em the next night, and Charlie Brice 'ad Mrs. Jennings all alone to himself for over a couple of hours walking up and down the Commercial Road talking about the weather; Charles saying 'ow wet and cold it, was, and thinking p'r'aps they 'ad better go off 'ome afore she got a chill.

He complained to Ted about it when 'e got 'ome, and Ted promised as it shouldn't 'appen agin. He said that 'im and Emma 'ad been so busy talking about getting married that he 'ad forgotten to keep an eye on him.

"Married!" ses Charlie, very upset. "Married! And wot's to become o' me?"

"Come and lodge with us," ses Ted.

They shook hands on it, but Ted said they 'ad both better keep it to themselves a bit and wait until Emma 'ad got more used to Charlie afore they told her. Ted let 'er get used to 'im for three days more afore he broke the news to 'er, and the way she went on was alarming. She went on for over ten minutes without taking breath, and she was just going to start again when Mrs. Jennings stopped her.

"He's all right," she ses. "You leave 'im alone."

"I'm not touching 'im," ses Emma, very scornful.

"You leave 'im alone," ses Mrs. Jennings, taking hold of Charlie's arm. "I don't say things about your young man."

Charlie Brice started as if he 'ad been shot, and twice he opened 'is mouth to speak and show Mrs. Jennings 'er mistake; but, wot with trying to find 'is voice in the fust place, and then finding words to use it with in the second, he didn't say anything. He just walked along gasping, with 'is mouth open like a fish.

"Don't take no notice of 'er, Charlie," ses Mrs. Jennings.

"I—I don't mind wot she ses," ses pore Charlie; "but you're making a great—"

"She's quick-tempered, is Emma," ses Mrs. Jennings. "But, there, so am I. Wot you might call a generous temper, but quick."

Charlie went cold all over.

"Treat me well and I treat other people well," ses Mrs. Jennings. "I can't say fairer than that, can I?"

Charlie said "Nobody could," and then 'e walked along with her hanging on to 'is arm, arf wondering whether it would be wrong to shove 'er under a bus that was passing, and arf wondering whether 'e could do it if it wasn't.

"As for Emma saying she won't 'ave you for a lodger," ses Mrs. Jennings, "let 'er wait till she's asked. She'll wait a long time if I 'ave my say."

Charlie didn't answer her. He walked along with 'is mouth shut, his idea being that the least said the soonest mended. Even Emma asked 'im at last whether he 'ad lost 'is tongue, and said it was curious 'ow different love took different people.

He talked fast enough going 'ome with Ted though, and pretty near lost 'is temper with 'im when Ted asked 'im why he didn't tell Mrs. Jennings straight that she 'ad made a mistake.

"She knows well enough," he says, grinding 'is teeth; "she was just trying it on. That's 'ow it is widders get married agin. You'll 'ave to choose between going out with me or Emma, Ted. I can't face Mrs. Jennings again. I didn't think anybody could 'ave parted us like that."

Ted said it was all nonsense, but it was no good, and the next night he went off alone and came back very cross, saying that Mrs. Jennings 'ad been with 'em all the time, and when 'e spoke to Emma about it she said it was just tit for tat, and reminded 'im 'ow she had 'ad to put up with Charlie. For four nights running 'e went out for walks, with Emma holding one of 'is arms and Mrs. Jennings the other.

"It's miserable for you all alone 'ere by yourself, Charlie," he ses. "Why not come? She can't marry you against your will. Besides, I miss you."

Charlie shook 'ands with 'im, but 'e said 'e wouldn't walk out with Mrs. Jennings for a fortune. And all that Ted could say made no difference. He stayed indoors of an evening reading the paper, or going for little walks by 'imself, until at last Ted came 'ome one evening, smiling all over his face, and told 'im they had both been making fools of themselves for nothing.

"Mrs. Jennings is going to be married," he ses, clapping Charlie on the back.

"*Wot?*" ses Charlie.

Ted nodded. "Her and Emma 'ad words to-night," he ses, laughing, "and it all come out. She's been keeping company for some time. He's away at present, and they're going to be married as soon as 'e comes back."

"Well," ses Charlie, "why did she—"

"To oblige Emma," ses Ted, "to frighten you into staying at 'ome. I'd 'ad my suspicions for some time, from one or two things I picked up."

"Ho!" ses Charlie. "Well, it'll be my turn to laugh to-morrow night. We'll see whether she can shake me off agin."

Ted looked at 'im a bit worried. "It's a bit orkard," he ses, speaking very slow. "You see, they made it up arterwards, and then they both made me promise not to tell you, and if you come, they'll know I 'ave."

Charlie did a bit o' thinking. "Not if I pretend to make love to Mrs. Jennings?" he ses, at last, winking at 'im. "And it'll serve her right for being deceitful. We'll see 'ow she likes it. Wot sort o' chap is the young man—big?"

"Can't be," ses Ted; "cos Emma called 'im a little shrimp."

"I'll come," ses Charlie; "and it'll be your own fault if they find out you told me about it."

They fell asleep talking of it, and the next evening Charlie put on a new neck-tie he 'ad bought, and arter letting Ted have arf an hour's start went out and met 'em accidental. The fust Mrs. Jennings knew of 'is being there was by finding an arm put round 'er waist.

"Good-evening, Sophy," he ses.

"'Ow—'ow dare you?" ses Mrs. Jennings, giving a scream and pushing him away.

Charlie looked surprised.

"Why, ain't you pleased to see me?" he ses. "I've 'ad the raging toothache for over a week; I've got it now a bit, but I couldn't stay away from you any longer."

"You behave yourself," ses Mrs. Jennings.

"Ted didn't say anything about your toothache," ses Emma.

"I wouldn't let 'im, for fear of alarming Sophy," ses Charlie.

Mrs. Jennings gave a sort of laugh and a sniff mixed.

"Ain't you pleased to see me agin?" ses Charlie.

"I don't want to see you," ses Mrs. Jennings. "Wot d'ye think I want to see you for?"

"Change your mind pretty quick, don't you?" ses Charlie. "It's blow 'ot and blow cold with you seemingly. Why, I've been counting the minutes till I should see you agin."

Mrs. Jennings told 'im not to make a fool of 'imself, and Charlie saw 'er look at Emma in a puzzled sort of way, as if she didn't know wot to make of it. She kept drawing away from 'im and he kept drawing close to 'er; other people on the pavement dodging and trying to get out of their way, and asking them which side they was going and to stick to it.

"Why don't you behave yourself?" ses Emma, at last.

"We're all right," ses Charlie; "you look arter your own young man. We can look arter ourselves."

"Speak for yourself," ses Mrs. Jennings, very sharp.

Charlie laughed, and the more Mrs. Jennings showed 'er dislike for 'is nonsense the more he gave way to it. Even Ted thought it was going too far, and tried to interfere when he put his arm round

Mrs. Jennings's waist and made 'er dance to a piano-organ; but there was no stopping 'im, and at last Mrs. Jennings said she had 'ad enough of it, and told Emma she was going off 'ome.

"Don't take no notice of 'im," ses Emma.

"I must," ses Mrs. Jennings, who was arf crying with rage.

"Well, if you go 'ome, I shall go," ses Emma. "I don't want 'is company. I believe he's doing it on purpose.

"Behave yourself, Charlie," ses Ted.

"All right, old man," ses Charlie. "You look arter your young woman and I'll look arter mine."

"Your wot?" ses Mrs. Jennings, very loud.

"My young woman," ses Charlie.

"Look 'ere," ses Emma. "You may as well know first as last—Sophy 'as got a young man."

"O' course she 'as," ses Charlie. "Twenty-seven on the second of next January, he is; same as me."

"She's going to be married," ses Emma, very solemn.

"Yes, to me," ses Charlie, pretending to be surprised. "Didn't you know that?"

He looked so pleased with 'imself at his cleverness that Emma arf put up her 'and, and then she thought better of it and turned away.

"He's just doing it to get rid of you," she ses to Mrs. Jennings, "and if you give way you're a bigger silly than I took you for. Let 'im go on and 'ave his own way, and tell your intended about 'im when you see 'im. Arter all, you started it."

"I was only 'aving a bit o' fun," ses Mrs. Jennings.

"Well, so is he," ses Emma.

"Not me!" ses Charlie, turning his eyes up. "I'm in dead earnest; and so is she. It's only shyness on 'er part; it'll soon wear off."

He took 'old of Mrs. Jennings's arm agin and began to tell 'er 'ow lonely 'is life was afore she came acrost his path like an angel that had lost its way. And he went on like that till she told Emma that she'd either 'ave to go off 'ome or scream. Ted interfered agin then, and, arter listening to wot he 'ad got to say, Charlie said as 'ow he'd try and keep his love under control a bit more.

"She won't stand much more of it," he ses to Ted, arter they 'ad got 'ome that night. "I shouldn't be surprised if she don't turn up to-morrow."

Ted shook his 'ead. "She'll turn up to oblige Emma," he ses; "but there's no need for you to overdo it, Charlie. If her young man 'appened to get to 'ear of it it might cause trouble."

"I ain't afraid of 'im," ses Charlie, "not if your description of 'im is right."

"Emma knows 'im," ses Ted, "and I know she don't think much of 'im. She says he ain't as big as I am."

Charlie smiled to himself and laid awake for a little while thinking of pet names to surprise Mrs. Jennings with. He called 'er a fresh one every night for a week, and every night he took 'er a little bunch o' flowers with 'is love. When she flung 'em on the pavement he pretended to think she 'ad dropped 'em; but, do wot he would, 'e couldn't frighten 'er into staying away, and 'is share of music-'alls and bus rides and things like that was more than 'e cared to think of. All the time Ted was as happy as a sand-boy, and one evening when Emma asked 'im to go 'ome to supper 'e was so pleased 'e could 'ardly speak.

"Father thought he'd like to see you," ses Emma. "I shall be proud to shake 'im by the 'and," ses Ted, going red with joy.

"And you're to come, too, Sophy," ses Emma, turning to Mrs. Jennings.

Charlie coughed, feeling a bit orkard-like, and Emma stood there as if waiting for 'im to go.

"Well, so long," ses Charlie at last. "Take care o' my little prize packet."

"You can come, too, if you like," ses Emma. "Father said I was to bring you. Don't 'ave none of your nonsense there, that's all."

Charlie thanked 'er, and they was all walking along, him and Mrs. Jennings behind, when Emma looked over 'er shoulder.

"Sophy's young man is coming," she ses.

"Ho!" ses Charlie. He walked along doing a bit o' thinking, and by and by 'e gives a little laugh, and he ses, "I—I don't think p'r'aps I'll come arter all."

"Afraid?" ses Emma, with a nasty laugh.

"No," ses Charlie.

"Well, it looks like it," ses Emma.

"He's brave enough where wimmen are concerned," ses Mrs. Jennings.

"I was thinking of you," ses Charlie.

"You needn't trouble about me," ses Mrs. Jennings. "I can look after myself, thank you."

Charlie looked round, but there was no help for it. He got as far away from Mrs. Jennings as possible, and when they got to Emma's house he went in last.

Emma's father and mother was there and two or three of 'er brothers and sisters, but the fust thing that Charlie noticed was a great lump of a man standing by the mantelpiece staring at 'im.

"Come in, and make yourselves at 'ome," ses Mr. White. "I'm glad to see you both. Emma 'as told me all about you."

Charlie's 'art went down into 'is boots, but every-body was so busy drawing their chairs up to the table that they didn't notice 'ow pale he 'ad gone. He sat between Mr. White and Mrs. Jennings, and by and by, when everybody was talking, he turned to 'im in a whisper, and asked 'im who the big chap was.

"Mrs. Jennings's brother," ses Mr. White; "brewer's drayman he is."

Charlie said, "Oh!" and went on eating, a bit relieved in 'is mind.

"Your friend and my gal 'll make a nice couple," ses Mr. White, looking at Ted and Emma, sitting 'and in 'and.

"She couldn't 'ave a better husband," ses Charlie, whispering again; "but where is Mrs. Jennings's young man? I 'eard he was to be here."

Mr. White put down 'is knife and fork. "Eh?" he ses, staring at 'im.

"Mrs. Jennings's intended?" ses Charlie.

"Who are you getting at?" ses Mr. White, winking at 'im.

"But she 'as got one, ain't she?" ses Charlie. "That'll do," ses Mr. White, with another wink. "Try it on somebody else."

"Wot are you two talking about?" ses Emma, who 'ad been watching 'em.

"He's trying to pull my leg," ses 'er father, smiling all over his face. "Been asking me where Mrs. Jennings's young man is. P'r'aps you oughtn't to 'ave told us yet, Emma."

"It's all right," ses Emma. "He's got a very jealous disposition, poor fellow; and me and Sophy have been telling 'im about a young man just to tease 'im. We've been describing him to 'imself all along, and he thought it was somebody else."

She caught Charlie's eye, and all in a flash he saw 'ow he 'ad been done. Some of 'em began to laugh, and Mrs. Jennings put her 'and on his and gave it a squeeze. He sat there struck all of a heap, wondering wot he was going to do, and just at that moment there was a knock at the street door.

"I'll open it," he ses.

He jumped up before anybody could stop 'im and went to the door. Two seconds arter Ted Denver followed 'im, and that is last he ever saw of Charlie Brice, he was running down the road without 'is hat as hard as he could run.

"What I want you to do," said Mr. George Wright, as he leaned towards the old sailor, "is to be an uncle to me."

"Aye, aye," said the mystified Mr. Kemp, pausing with a mug of beer midway to his lips.

"A rich uncle," continued the young man, lowering his voice to prevent any keen ears in the next bar from acquiring useless knowledge. "An uncle from New Zealand, who is going to leave me all 'is money."

"Where's it coming from?" demanded Mr. Kemp, with a little excitement.

"It ain't coming," was the reply. "You've only got to say you've got it. Fact of the matter is, I've got my eye on a young lady; there's another chap after 'er too, and if she thought I'd got a rich uncle it might make all the difference. She knows I 'ad an uncle that went to New Zealand and was never heard of since. That's what made me think of it."

Mr. Kemp drank his beer in thoughtful silence. "How can I be a rich uncle without any brass?" he inquired at length.

"I should 'ave to lend you some—a little," said Mr. Wright.

The old man pondered. "I've had money lent me before," he said, candidly, "but I can't call to mind ever paying it back. I always meant to, but that's as far as it got."

"It don't matter," said the other. "It'll only be for a little while, and then you'll 'ave a letter calling you back to New Zealand. See? And you'll go back, promising to come home in a year's time, after you've wound up your business, and leave us all your money. See?"

Mr. Kemp scratched the back of his neck. "But she's sure to find it out in time," he objected.

"P'r'aps," said Mr. Wright. "And p'r'aps not. There'll be plenty of time for me to get married before she does, and you could write back and say you had got married yourself, or given your money to a hospital."

He ordered some more beer for Mr. Kemp, and in a low voice gave him as much of the family history as he considered necessary.

"I've only known you for about ten days," he concluded, "but I'd sooner trust you than people I've known for years."

"I took a fancy to you the moment I set eyes on you," rejoined Mr. Kemp. "You're the living image of a young fellow that lent me five pounds once, and was drowned afore my eyes the week after. He 'ad a bit of a squint, and I s'pose that's how he came to fall overboard."

He emptied his mug, and then, accompanied by Mr. Wright, fetched his sea-chest from the boarding-house where he was staying, and took it to the young man's lodgings. Fortunately for the latter's pocket the chest contained a good best suit and boots, and the only expenses incurred were for a large, soft felt hat and a gilded watch and chain. Dressed in his best, with a bulging pocket-book in his breast-pocket, he set out with Mr. Wright on the following evening to make his first call.

Mr. Wright, who was also in his best clothes, led the way to a small tobacconist's in a side street off the Mile End Road, and, raising his hat with some ceremony, shook hands with a good-looking young woman who stood behind the counter: Mr. Kemp, adopting an air of scornful dignity intended to indicate the possession of great wealth, waited.

"This is my uncle," said Mr. Wright, speaking rapidly, "from New Zealand, the one I spoke to you about. He turned up last night, and you might have knocked me down with a feather. The last person in the world I expected to see."

Mr. Kemp, in a good rolling voice, said, "Good evening, miss; I hope you are well," and, subsiding into a chair, asked for a cigar. His surprise when he found that the best cigar they stocked only cost sixpence almost assumed the dimensions of a grievance.

"It'll do to go on with," he said, smelling it suspiciously. "Have you got change for a fifty-pound note?"

Miss Bradshaw, concealing her surprise by an effort, said that she would see, and was scanning the contents of a drawer, when Mr. Kemp in some haste discovered a few odd sovereigns in his waistcoat-pocket. Five minutes later he was sitting in the little room behind the shop, holding forth to an admiring audience.

"So far as I know," he said, in reply to a question of Mrs. Bradshaw's, "George is the only relation I've got. Him and me are quite alone, and I can tell you I was glad to find him."

Mrs. Bradshaw sighed. "It's a pity you are so far apart," she said.

"It's not for long," said Mr. Kemp. "I'm just going back for about a year to wind up things out there, and then I'm coming back to leave my old bones over here. George has very kindly offered to let me live with him."

"He won't suffer for it, I'll be bound," said Mrs. Bradshaw, archly.

"So far as money goes he won't," said the old man. "Not that that would make any difference to George."

"It would be the same to me if you hadn't got a farthing," said Mr. Wright, promptly.

Mr. Kemp, somewhat affected, shook hands with him, and leaning back in the most comfortable chair in the room, described his life and struggles in New Zealand. Hard work, teetotalism, and the simple life combined appeared to be responsible for a fortune which he affected to be too old to enjoy. Misunderstandings of a painful nature were avoided by a timely admission that under medical advice he was now taking a fair amount of stimulant.

"Mind," he said, as he walked home with the elated George, "it's your game, not mine, and it's sure to come a bit expensive. I can't be a rich uncle without spending a bit. 'Ow much did you say you'd got in the bank?"

"We must be as careful as we can," said Mr. Wright, hastily. "One thing is they can't leave the shop to go out much. It's a very good little business, and it ought to be all right for me and Bella one of these days, eh?"

Mr. Kemp, prompted by a nudge in the ribs, assented. "It's wonderful how they took it all in about me," he said; "but I feel certain in my own mind that I ought to chuck some money about."

"Tell 'em of the money you have chucked about," said Mr. Wright. "It'll do just as well, and come a good deal cheaper. And you had better go round alone to-morrow evening. It'll look better. Just go in for another one of their sixpenny cigars."

Mr. Kemp obeyed, and the following evening, after sitting a little while chatting in the shop, was invited into the parlour, where, mindful of Mr. Wright's instructions, he held his listeners enthralled by tales of past expenditure. A tip of fifty pounds to his bedroom steward coming over was characterized by Mrs. Bradshaw as extravagant.

"Seems to be going all right," said Mr. Wright, as the old man made his report; "but be careful; don't go overdoing it."

Mr. Kemp nodded. "I can turn 'em round my little finger," he said. "You'll have Bella all to yourself to-morrow evening."

Mr. Wright flushed. "How did you manage that?" he inquired. "It's the first time she has ever been out with me alone."

"She ain't coming out," said Mr. Kemp. "She's going to stay at home and mind the shop; it's the mother what's coming out. Going to spend the evening with me!"

Mr. Wright frowned. "What did you do that for?" he demanded, hotly.

"I didn't do it," said Mr. Kemp, equably; "they done it. The old lady says that, just for once in her life, she wants to see how it feels to spend money like water."

"*Money like water!*" repeated the horrified Mr. Wright. "Money like— I'll 'money' her—I'll—"

"It don't matter to me," said Mr. Kemp. "I can have a headache or a chill, or something of that sort, if you like. I don't want to go. It's no pleasure to me."

"What will it cost?" demanded Mr. Wright, pacing up and down the room.

The rich uncle made a calculation. "She wants to go to a place called the Empire," he said, slowly, "and have something for supper, and there'd be cabs and things. I dessay it would cost a couple o' pounds, and it might be more. But I'd just as soon ave' a chill—just."

Mr. Wright groaned, and after talking of Mrs. Bradshaw as though she were already his mother-in-law, produced the money. His instructions as to economy lasted almost up to the moment when he stood with Bella outside the shop on the following evening and watched the couple go off.

"It's wonderful how well they get on together," said Bella, as they re-entered the shop and passed into the parlour. "I've never seen mother take to anybody so quick as she has to him."

"I hope you like him, too," said Mr. Wright.

"He's a dear," said Bella. "Fancy having all that money. I wonder what it feels like?"

"I suppose I shall know some day," said the young man, slowly; "but it won't be much good to me unless—"

"Unless?" said Bella, after a pause.

"Unless it gives me what I want," replied the other. "I'd sooner be a poor man and married to the girl I love, than a millionaire."

Miss Bradshaw stole an uneasy glance at his somewhat sallow features, and became thoughtful.

"It's no good having diamonds and motor-cars and that sort of thing unless you have somebody to share them with," pursued Mr. Wright.

Miss Bradshaw's eyes sparkled, and at that moment the shop-bell tinkled and a lively whistle sounded. She rose and went into the shop, and Mr. Wright settled back in his chair and scowled darkly as he saw the intruder.

"Good evening," said the latter. "I want a sixpenny smoke for twopence, please. How are we this evening? Sitting up and taking nourishment?"

Miss Bradshaw told him to behave himself.

"Always do," said the young man. "That's why I can never get anybody to play with. I had such an awful dream about you last night that I couldn't rest till I saw you. Awful it was."

"What was it?" inquired Miss Bradshaw.

"Dreamt you were married," said Mr. Hills, smiling at her.

Miss Bradshaw tossed her head. "Who to, pray?" she inquired.

"Me," said Mr. Hills, simply. "I woke up in a cold perspiration. Halloa! is that Georgie in there? How are you, George? Better?"

"I'm all right," said Mr. Wright, with dignity, as the other hooked the door open with his stick and nodded at him.

"Well, why don't you look it?" demanded the lively Mr. Hills. "Have you got your feet wet, or what?"

"Oh, be quiet," said Miss Bradshaw, smiling at him.

"Right-o," said Mr. Hills, dropping into a chair by the counter and caressing his moustache. "But you wouldn't speak to me like that if you knew what a terrible day I've had."

"What have you been doing?" asked the girl.

"Working," said the other, with a huge sigh. "Where's the millionaire? I came round on purpose to have a look at him."

"Him and mother have gone to the Empire?" said Miss Bradshaw.

Mr. Hills gave three long, penetrating whistles, and then, placing his cigar with great care on the counter, hid his face in a huge handkerchief. Miss Bradshaw, glanced from him to the frowning Mr. Wright, and then, entering the parlour, closed the door with a bang. Mr. Hills took the hint, and with a somewhat thoughtful grin departed.

He came in next evening for another cigar, and heard all that there was to hear about the Empire. Mrs. Bradshaw would have treated him but coldly, but the innocent Mr. Kemp, charmed by his manner, paid him great attention.

"He's just like what I was at his age," he said. "Lively."

"I'm not a patch on you," said Mr. Hills, edging his way by slow degrees into the parlour. "I don't take young ladies to the Empire. Were you telling me you came over here to get married, or did I dream it?"

"'Ark at him," said the blushing Mr. Kemp, as Mrs. Bradshaw shook her head at the offender and told him to behave himself.

"He's a man any woman might be happy with," said Mr. Hills. "He never knows how much there is in his trousers-pocket. Fancy sewing on buttons for a man like that. Gold-mining ain't in it."

Mrs. Bradshaw shook her head at him again, and Mr. Hills, after apologizing to her for revealing her innermost thoughts before the most guileless of men, began to question Mr. Kemp as to the prospects of a bright and energetic young man, with a distaste for work, in New Zealand. The audience listened with keen attention to the replies, the only disturbing factor being a cough of Mr. Wright's, which became more and more troublesome as the evening wore on. By the time uncle and nephew rose to depart the latter was so hoarse that he could scarcely speak.

"Why didn't you tell 'em you had got a letter calling you home, as I told you?" he vociferated, as soon as they were clear of the shop.

"I—I forgot it," said the old man.

"Forgot it!" repeated the incensed Mr. Wright.

"What did you think I was coughing like that for—fun?"

"I forgot it," said the old man, doggedly. "Besides, if you take my advice, you'd better let me stay a little longer to make sure of things."

Mr. Wright laughed disagreeably. "I dare say," he said; "but I am managing this affair, not you. Now, you go round to-morrow afternoon and tell them you're off. D'ye hear? D'ye think I'm made of money? And what do you mean by making such a fuss of that fool, Charlie Hills? You know he is after Bella."

He walked the rest of the way home in indignant silence, and, after giving minute instructions to Mr. Kemp next morning at breakfast, went off to work in a more cheerful frame of mind. Mr. Kemp was out when he returned, and after making his toilet he followed him to Mrs. Bradshaw's.

To his annoyance, he found Mr. Hills there again; and, moreover, it soon became clear to him that Mr. Kemp had said nothing about his approaching departure. Coughs and scowls passed unheeded, and at last in a hesitating voice, he broached the subject himself. There was a general chorus of lamentation.

"I hadn't got the heart to tell you," said Mr. Kemp. "I don't know when I've been so happy."

"But you haven't got to go back immediate," said Mrs. Bradshaw.

"To-morrow," said Mr. Wright, before the old man could reply. "Business."

"Must you go," said Mrs. Bradshaw.

Mr. Kemp smiled feebly. "I suppose I ought to," he replied, in a hesitating voice.

"Take my tip and give yourself a bit of a holiday before you go back," urged Mr. Hills.

"Just for a few days," pleaded Bella.

"To please us," said Mrs. Bradshaw. "Think 'ow George'll miss you."

"Lay hold of him and don't let him go," said Mr. Hills.

He took Mr. Kemp round the waist, and the laughing Bella and her mother each secured an arm. An appeal to Mr. Wright to secure his legs passed unheeded.

"We don't let you go till you promise," said Mrs. Bradshaw.

Mr. Kemp smiled and shook his head. "Promise?" said Bella.

"Well, well," said Mr. Kemp; "p'r'aps—"

"He must go back," shouted the alarmed Mr. Wright.

"Let him speak for himself," exclaimed Bella, indignantly.

"Just another week then," said Mr. Kemp. "It's no good having money if I can't please myself."

"A week!" shouted Mr. Wright, almost beside himself with rage and dismay. "A week! Another week! Why, you told me—"

"Oh, don't listen to him," said Mrs. Bradshaw. "Croaker! It's his own business, ain't it? And he knows best, don't he? What's it got to do with you?"

She patted Mr. Kemp's hand; Mr. Kemp patted back, and with his disengaged hand helped himself to a glass of beer—the fourth—and beamed in a friendly fashion upon the company.

"George!" he said, suddenly.

"Yes," said Mr. Wright, in a harsh voice.

"Did you think to bring my pocket-book along with you?"

"No," said Mr. Wright, sharply; "I didn't."

"Tt-tt," said the old man, with a gesture of annoyance. "Well, lend me a couple of pounds, then, or else run back and fetch my pocket-book," he added, with a sly grin.

Mr. Wright's face worked with impotent fury. "What—what—do you—want it for?" he gasped.

Mrs. Bradshaw's "Well! Well!" seemed to sum up the general feeling; Mr. Kemp, shaking his head, eyed him with gentle reproach.

"Me and Mrs. Bradshaw are going to gave another evening out," he said, quietly. "I've only got a few more days, and I must make hay while the sun shines."

To Mr. Wright the room seemed to revolve slowly on its axis, but, regaining his self-possession by a supreme effort, he took out his purse and produced the amount. Mrs. Bradshaw, after a few feminine protestations, went upstairs to put her bonnet on.

"And you can go and fetch a hansom-cab, George, while she's a-doing of it," said Mr. Kemp. "Pick out a good 'orse—spotted-grey, if you can."

Mr. Wright arose and, departing with a suddenness that was almost startling, exploded harmlessly in front of the barber's, next door but one. Then with lagging steps he went in search of the shabbiest cab and oldest horse he could find.

"Thankee, my boy," said Mr. Kemp, bluffly, as he helped Mrs. Bradshaw in and stood with his foot on the step. "By the way, you had better go back and lock my pocket-book up. I left it on the washstand, and there's best part of a thousand pounds in it. You can take fifty for yourself to buy smokes with."

There was a murmur of admiration, and Mr. Wright, with a frantic attempt to keep up appearances, tried to thank him, but in vain. Long after the cab had rolled away he stood on the pavement trying to think out a position which was rapidly becoming unendurable. Still keeping up appearances, he had to pretend to go home to look after the pocket-book, leaving the jubilant Mr. Hills to improve the shining hour with Miss Bradshaw.

Mr. Kemp, returning home at midnight—in a cab—found the young man waiting up for him, and, taking a seat on the edge of the table, listened unmoved to a word-picture of himself which seemed interminable. He was only moved to speech when Mr. Wright described him as a white-whiskered jezebel who was a disgrace to his sex, and then merely in the interests of natural science.

"Don't you worry," he said, as the other paused from exhaustion. "It won't be for long now."

"Long?" said Mr. Wright, panting. "First thing to-morrow morning you have a telegram calling you back—a telegram that must be minded. D'ye see?"

"No, I don't," said Mr. Kemp, plainly. "I'm not going back, never no more—never! I'm going to stop here and court Mrs. Bradshaw."

Mr. Wright fought for breath. "You—you can't!" he gasped.

"I'm going to have a try," said the old man. "I'm sick of going to sea, and it'll be a nice comfortable home for my old age. You marry Bella, and I'll marry her mother. Happy family!"

Mr. Wright, trembling with rage, sat down to recover, and, regaining his composure after a time, pointed out almost calmly the various difficulties in the way.

"I've thought it all out," said Mr. Kemp, nodding. "She mustn't know I'm not rich till after we're married; then I 'ave a letter from New Zealand saying I've lost all my money. It's just as easy to have that letter as the one you spoke of."

"And I'm to find you money to play the rich uncle with till you're married, I suppose," said Mr. Wright, in a grating voice, "and then lose Bella when Mrs. Bradshaw finds you've lost your money?"

Mr. Kemp scratched his ear. "That's your lookout," he said, at last.

"Now, look here," said Mr. Wright, with great determination. "Either you go and tell them that you've been telegraphed for—cabled is the proper word—or I tell them the truth."

"That'll settle you then," said Mr. Kemp.

"No more than the other would," retorted the young man, "and it'll come cheaper. One thing I'll take my oath of, and that is I won't give you another farthing; but if you do as I tell you I'll give you a quid for luck. Now, think it over."

Mr. Kemp thought it over, and after a vain attempt to raise the promised reward to five pounds, finally compounded for two, and went off to bed after a few stormy words on selfishness and ingratitude. He declined to speak to his host at breakfast next morning, and accompanied him in the evening with the air of a martyr going to the stake. He listened in stony silence to the young man's instructions, and only spoke when the latter refused to pay the two pounds in advance.

The news, communicated in halting accents by Mr. Kemp, was received with flattering dismay. Mrs. Bradshaw refused to believe her ears, and it was only after the information had been repeated and confirmed by Mr. Wright that she understood.

"I must go," said Mr. Kemp. "I've spent over eleven pounds cabling to-day; but it's all no good."

"But you're coming back?" said Mr. Hills.

"O' course I am," was the reply. "George is the only relation I've got, and I've got to look after him, I suppose. After all, blood is thicker than water."

"Hear, hear!" said Mrs. Bradshaw, piously.

"And there's you and Bella," continued Mr. Kemp; "two of the best that ever breathed."

The ladies looked down.

"And Charlie Hills; I don't know—I don't know *when* I've took such a fancy to anybody as I have to 'im. If I was a young gal—a single young gal—he's—the other half," he said, slowly, as he paused—"just the one I should fancy. He's a good-'arted, good-looking—"

"Draw it mild," interrupted the blushing Mr. Hills as Mr. Wright bestowed a ferocious glance upon the speaker.

"Clever, lively young fellow," concluded Mr. Kemp. "George!"

"Yes," said Mr. Wright.

"I'm going now. I've got to catch the train for Southampton, but I don't want you to come with me. I prefer to be alone. You stay here and cheer them up. Oh, and before I forget it, lend me a couple o' pounds out o' that fifty I gave you last night. I've given all my small change away."

He looked up and met Mr. Wright's eye; the latter, too affected to speak, took out the money and passed it over.

"We never know what may happen to us," said the old man, solemnly, as he rose and buttoned his coat. "I'm an old man and I like to have things ship-shape. I've spent nearly the whole day with my lawyer, and if anything 'appens to my old carcass it won't make any difference. I have left half my money to George; half of all I have is to be his."

In the midst of an awed silence he went round and shook hands.

"The other half," with his hand on the door—"the other half and my best gold watch and chain I have left to my dear young pal, Charlie Hills. Good-bye, Georgie!"

OUTSAILED

It was a momentous occasion. The two skippers sat in the private bar of the "Old Ship," in High Street, Wapping, solemnly sipping cold gin and smoking cigars, whose sole merit consisted in the fact that they had been smuggled. It is well known all along the waterside that this greatly improves their flavour.

"Draw all right?" queried Captain Berrow?-a short, fat man of few ideas, who was the exulting owner of a bundle of them.

"Beautiful," replied Captain Tucker, who had just made an excursion into the interior of his with the small blade of his penknife. "Why don't you keep smokes like these, landlord?"

"He can't," chuckled Captain Berrow fatuously. "They're not to be 'ad—money couldn't buy 'em."

The landlord grunted. "Why don't you settle about that race o' yours an' ha' done with it," he cried, as he wiped down his counter. "Seems to me, Cap'n Tucker's hanging fire."

"I'm ready when he is," said Tucker, somewhat shortly.

"It's taking your money," said Berrow slowly; "the Thistle can't hold a candle to the Good Intent, and you know it. Many a time that little schooner o' mine has kept up with a steamer."

"Wher'd you ha' been if the tow rope had parted, though?" said the master of the Thistle, with a wink at the landlord.

At this remark Captain Berrow took fire, and, with his temper rapidly rising to fever heat, wrathfully repelled the scurvy insinuation in language which compelled the respectful attention of all the other customers and the hasty intervention of the landlord.

"Put up the stakes," he cried impatiently. "Put up the stakes, and don't have so much jaw about it."

"Here's mine," said Berrow, sturdily handing over a greasy fiver. "Now, Cap'n Tucker, cover that."

"Come on," said the landlord encouragingly; "don't let him take the wind out of your sails like that."

Tucker handed over five sovereigns.

"High water's at 12.13," said the landlord, pocketing the stakes. "You understand the conditions?- each of you does the best he can for hisself after eleven, an' the one what gets to Poole first has the ten quid. Understand?"

Both gamblers breathed hard, and, fully realising the desperate nature of the enterprise upon which they had embarked, ordered some more gin. A rivalry of long standing as to the merits of their respective schooners had led to them calling in the landlord to arbitrate, and this was the result. Berrow, vaguely feeling that it would be advisable to keep on good terms with the stakeholder, offered him one of the famous cigars. The stakeholder, anxious to keep on good terms with his stomach, declined it.

"You've both got your moorings up, I s'pose?" he inquired.

"Got 'em up this evening," replied Tucker. "We're just made fast one on each side of the Dolphin now."

"The wind's light, but it's from the right quarter," said Captain Berrow, "an' I only hope as 'ow the best ship'll win. I'd like to win myself, but, if not, I can only say as there's no man breathing I'd sooner have lick me than Cap'n Tucker. He's as smart a seaman as ever comes into the London river, an' he's got a schooner angels would be proud of."

"Glasses o' gin round," said Tucker promptly. "Cap'n Berrow, here's your very good health, an' a fair field an' no favour."

With these praiseworthy sentiments the master of the Thistle finished his liquor, and, wiping his mouth on the back of his hand, nodded farewell to the twain and departed. Once in the High Street he walked slowly, as one in deep thought, then, with a sudden resolution, turned up Nightingale Lane, and made for a small, unsavoury thoroughfare leading out of Ratcliff Highway. A quarter of an hour later he emerged into that famous thoroughfare again, smiling incoherently, and, retracing his steps to the waterside, jumped into a boat, and was pulled off to his ship.

"Comes off to-night, Joe," said he, as he descended to the cabin, "an' it's arf a quid to you if the old gal wins."

"What's the bet?" inquired the mate, looking up from his task of shredding tobacco.

"Five quid," replied the skipper.

"Well, we ought to do it," said the mate slowly; "'t wont be my fault if we don't."

"Mine neither," said the skipper. "As a matter o' fact, Joe, I reckon I've about made sure of it. All's fair in love and war and racing, Joe."

"Ay, ay," said the mate, more slowly than before, as he revolved this addition to the proverb.

"I just nipped round and saw a chap I used to know named Dibbs," said the skipper. "Keeps a boarding-house for sailors. Wonderful sharp little chap he is. Needles ain't nothing to him. There's heaps of needles, but only one Dibbs. He's going to make old Berrow's chaps as drunk as lords."

"Does he know 'em?" inquired the mate.

"He knows where to find 'em," said the other. "I told him they'd either be in the 'Duke's Head' or the 'Town o' Berwick.' But he'd find 'em wherever they was. Ah, even if they was in a coffee pallis, I b'leeve that man 'ud find 'em."

"They're steady chaps," objected the mate, but in a weak fashion, being somewhat staggered by this tribute to Mr. Dibbs' remarkable powers.

"My lad," said the skipper, "it's Dibbs' business to mix sailors' liquors so's they don't know whether they're standing on their heads or their heels. He's the most wonderful mixer in Christendom; takes a reg'lar pride in it. Many a sailorman has got up a ship's side, thinking it was stairs, and gone off half acrost the world instead of going to bed, through him."

"We'll have a easy job of it, then," said the mate. "I b'leeve we could ha' managed it without that, though. 'Tain't quite what you'd call sport, is it?"

"There's nothing like making sure of a thing," said the skipper placidly. "What time's our chaps coming aboard?"

"Ten thirty, the latest," replied the mate. "Old Sam's with 'em, so they'll be all right."

"I'll turn in for a couple of hours," said the skipper, going towards his berth. "Lord! I'd give something to see old Berrow's face as his chaps come up the side."

"P'raps they won't git as far as that," remarked the mate.

"Oh, yes they will," said the skipper. "Dibbs is going to see to that. I don't want any chance of the race being scratched. Turn me out in a couple of hours."

He closed the door behind him, and the mate, having stuffed his clay with the coarse tobacco, took some pink note-paper with scalloped edges from his drawer, and, placing the paper at his right side, and squaring his shoulders, began some private correspondence.

For some time he smoked and wrote in silence, until the increasing darkness warned him to finish his task. He signed the note, and, having put a few marks of a tender nature below his signature, sealed it ready for the post, and sat with half-closed eyes, finishing his pipe. Then his head nodded, and, placing his arms on the table, he too slept.

It seemed but a minute since he had closed his eyes when he was awakened by the entrance of the skipper, who came blundering into the darkness from his stateroom, vociferating loudly and nervously.

"Ay, ay!" said Joe, starting up.

"Where's the lights?" said the skipper. "What's the time? I dreamt I'd overslept myself. What's the time?"

"Plenty o' time," said the mate vaguely, as he stifled a yawn.

"Ha'-past ten," said the skipper, as he struck a match, "You've been asleep," he added severely.

"I ain't," said the mate stoutly, as he followed the other on deck. "I've been thinking. I think better in the dark."

"It's about time our chaps was aboard," said the skipper, as he looked round the deserted deck. "I hope they won't be late."

"Sam's with 'em," said the mate confidently, as he went on to the side; "there ain't no festivities going on aboard the Good Intent, neither."

"There will be," said his worthy skipper, with a grin, as he looked across the intervening brig at the rival craft; "there will be."

He walked round the deck to see that everything was snug and ship-shape, and got back to the mate just as a howl of surprising weirdness was heard proceeding from the neighbouring stairs.

"I'm s'prised at Berrow allowing his men to make that noise," said the skipper waggishly. "Our chaps are there too, I think. I can hear Sam's voice."

"So can I," said the mate, with emphasis.

"Seems to be talking rather loud," said the master of the Thistle, knitting his brows.

"Sounds as though he's trying to sing," said the mate, as, after some delay, a heavily-laden boat put off from the stairs and made slowly for them. "No, he ain't; he's screaming."

There was no longer any doubt about it. The respectable and greatly-trusted Sam was letting off a series of wild howls which would have done credit to a penny-gaff Zulu, and was evidently very much out of temper about something.

"Ahoy, Thistle! Ahoy!" bellowed the waterman, as he neared the schooner. "Chuck us a rope?-quick!"

The mate threw him one, and the boat came alongside. It was then seen that another waterman, using impatient and deplorable language, was forcibly holding Sam down in the boat.

"What's he done? What's the row?" demanded the mate.

"Done?" said the waterman, in disgust. "Done? He's 'ad a small lemon, an' it's got into his silly old head. He's making all this fuss 'cos he wanted to set the pub on fire, an' they wouldn't let him. Man ashore told us they belonged to the Good Intent, but I know they're your men."

"Sam!" roared the skipper, with a sinking heart, as his glance fell on the recumbent figures in the boat; "come aboard at once, you drunken disgrace! D'ye hear?"

"I can't leave him," said Sam, whimpering.

"Leave who?" growled the skipper.

"Him," said Sam, placing his arms round the waterman's neck. "Him an' me's like brothers."

"Get up, you old loonatic!" snarled the waterman, extricating himself with difficulty, and forcing the other towards the side. "Now, up you go!"

Aided by the shoulders of the waterman and the hands of his superior officers, Sam went up, and then the waterman turned his attention to the remainder of his fares, who were snoring contentedly in the bottom of the boat.

"Now, then!" he cried; "look alive with you! D'ye hear? Wake up! Wake up! Kick 'em, Bill!"

"I can't kick no 'arder," grumbled the other waterman.

"What the devil's the matter with 'em?" stormed the master of the Thistle, "Chuck a pail of water over 'em, Joe!"

Joe obeyed with gusto; and, as he never had much of a head for details, bestowed most of it upon the watermen. Through the row which ensued the Thistle's crew snored peacefully, and at last were handed up over the sides like sacks of potatoes, and the indignant watermen pulled back to the stairs.

"Here's a nice crew to win a race with!" wailed the skipper, almost crying with rage. "Chuck the water over 'em, Joe! Chuck the water over 'em !"

Joe obeyed willingly, until at length, to the skipper's great relief, one man stirred, and, sitting up on the deck, sleepily expressed his firm conviction that it was raining. For a moment they both had hopes of him, but as Joe went to the side for another bucketful, he evidently came to the conclusion that he had been dreaming, and, lying down again, resumed his nap. As he did so the first stroke of Big Ben came booming down the river.

"Eleven o'clock!" shouted the excited skipper.

It was too true. Before Big Ben had finished, the neighbouring church clocks commenced striking with feverish haste, and hurrying feet and hoarse cries were heard proceeding from the deck of the GOOD INTENT.

"Loose the sails!" yelled the furious Tucker. "Loose the sails! Damme, we'll get under way by ourselves!"

He ran forward, and, assisted by the mate, hoisted the jibs, and then, running back, cast off from the brig, and began to hoist the mainsail. As they disengaged themselves from the tier, there was just sufficient sail for them to advance against the tide; while in front of them the Good Intent, shaking out sail after sail, stood boldly down the river.

"This was the way of it," said Sam, as he stood before the grim Tucker at six o'clock the next morning, surrounded by his mates. "He came into the 'Town o' Berwick,' where we was, as nice a spoken little chap as ever you'd wish to see. He said he'd been a-looking at the GOOD INTENT, and he thought it was the prettiest little craft 'e ever seed, and the exact image of one his dear brother, which was a missionary, 'ad, and he'd like to stand a drink to every man of her crew. Of course, we all said we was the crew direckly, an' all I can remember after that is two coppers an' a little boy trying to giv' me the frog's march, an' somebody chucking pails o' water over me. It's crool 'ard losing a race, what we didn't know nothink about, in this way; but it warn't our fault?-it warn't, indeed. It's my belief that the little man was a missionary of some sort hisself, and wanted to convert us, an' that was his way of starting on the job. It's all very well for the mate to have highstirriks; but it's quite true, every word of it, an' if you go an' ask at the pub they'll tell you the same."

OVER THE SIDE

Of all classes of men, those who follow the sea are probably the most prone to superstition. Afloat upon the black waste of waters, at the mercy of wind and sea, with vast depths and strange creatures below them, a belief in the supernatural is easier than ashore, under the cheerful gas-lamps. Strange stories of the sea are plentiful, and an incident which happened within my own experience has made me somewhat chary of dubbing a man fool or coward because he has encountered something he cannot explain. There are stories of the supernatural with prosaic sequels; there are others to which the sequel has never been published.

I was fifteen years old at the time, and as my father, who had a strong objection to the sea, would not apprentice me to it, I shipped before the mast on a sturdy little brig called the *Endeavour,* bound for Riga. She was a small craft, but the skipper was as fine a seaman as one could wish for, and, in fair weather, an easy man to sail under. Most boys have a rough time of it when they first go to sea, but, with a strong sense of what was good for me, I had attached myself to a brawny, good-natured infant, named Bill Smith, and it was soon understood that whoever hit me struck Bill by proxy. Not that the crew were particularly brutal, but a sound cuffing occasionally is held by most seamen to be beneficial to a lad's health and morals. The only really spiteful fellow among them was a man named Jem Dadd. He was a morose, sallow-looking man, of about forty, with a strong taste for the supernatural, and a stronger taste still for frightening his fellows with it. I have seen Bill almost afraid to go on deck of a night for his trick at the wheel, after a few of his reminiscences. Rats were a favourite topic with him, and he would never allow one to be killed if he could help it, for he claimed for them that they were the souls of drowned sailors, hence their love of ships and their habit of leaving them when they became unseaworthy. He was a firm believer in the transmigration of souls, some idea of which he had, no doubt, picked up in Eastern ports, and gave his shivering auditors to understand that his arrangements for his own immediate future were already perfected.

We were six or seven days out when a strange thing happened. Dadd had the second watch one night, and Bill was to relieve him. They were not very strict aboard the brig in fair weather, and when a man's time was up he just made the wheel fast, and, running for'ard, shouted down the fo'c's'le. On this night I happened to awake suddenly, in time to see Bill slip out of his bunk and stand by me, rubbing his red eyelids with his knuckles.

"Dadd's giving me a long time," he whispered, seeing that I was awake; "it's a whole hour after his time."

He pattered up on deck, and I was just turning over, thankful that I was too young to have a watch to keep, when he came softly down again, and, taking me by the shoulders, shook me roughly.

"Jack," he whispered. "Jack."

I raised myself on my elbows, and, in the light of the smoking lamp, saw that he was shaking all over.

"Come on deck," he said, thickly.

I put on my clothes, and followed him quietly to the sweet, cool air above. It was a beautiful clear night, but, from his manner, I looked nervously around for some cause of alarm. I saw nothing. The deck was deserted, except for the solitary figure at the wheel.

"Look at him," whispered Bill, bending a contorted face to mine.

I walked aft a few steps, and Bill followed slowly. Then I saw that Jem Dadd was leaning forward clumsily on the wheel, with his hands clenched on the spokes.

"He's asleep," said I, stopping short.

Bill breathed hard. "He's in a queer sleep," said he; "kind o' trance more like. Go closer."

I took fast hold of Bill's sleeve, and we both went. The light of the stars was sufficient to show that Dadd's face was very white, and that his dim, black eyes were wide open, and staring in a very strange and dreadful manner straight before him.

"Dadd," said I, softly, "Dadd!"

There was no reply, and, with a view of arousing him, I tapped one sinewy hand as it gripped the wheel, and even tried to loosen it.

He remained immovable, and, suddenly with a great cry, my courage deserted me, and Bill and I fairly bolted down into the cabin and woke the skipper.

Then we saw how it was with Jem, and two strong seamen forcibly loosened the grip of those rigid fingers, and, laying him on the deck, covered him with a piece of canvas. The rest of the night two men stayed at the wheel, and, gazing fearfully at the outline of the canvas, longed for dawn.

It came at last, and, breakfast over, the body was sewn up in canvas, and the skipper held a short service compiled from a Bible which belonged to the mate, and what he remembered of the Burial Service proper. Then the corpse went overboard with a splash, and the men, after standing awkwardly together for a few minutes, slowly dispersed to their duties.

For the rest of that day we were all very quiet and restrained; pity for the dead man being mingled with a dread of taking the wheel when night came.

"The wheel's haunted," said the cook, solemnly; "mark my words, there's more of you will be took the same way Dadd was."

The cook, like myself, had no watch to keep.

The men bore up pretty well until night came on again, and then they unanimously resolved to have a double watch. The cook, sorely against his will, was impressed into the service, and I, glad to oblige my patron, agreed to stay up with Bill.

Some of the pleasure had vanished by the time night came, and I seemed only just to have closed my eyes when Bill came, and, with a rough shake or two, informed me that the time had come. Any hope that I might have had of escaping the ordeal was at once dispelled by his expectant demeanour, and the helpful way in which he assisted me with my clothes, and, yawning terribly, I followed him on deck.

The night was not so clear as the preceding one, and the air was chilly, with a little moisture in it. I buttoned up my jacket, and thrust my hands in my pockets.

"Everything quiet?" asked Bill as he stepped up and took the wheel.

"Ay, ay," said Roberts, "quiet as the grave," and, followed by his willing mate, he went below.

I sat on the deck by Bill's side as, with a light touch on the wheel, he kept the brig to her course. It was weary work sitting there, doing nothing, and thinking of the warm berth below, and I believe that I should have fallen asleep, but that my watchful companion stirred me with his foot whenever he saw me nodding.

I suppose I must have sat there, shivering and yawning, for about an hour, when, tired of inactivity, I got up and went and leaned over the side of the vessel. The sound of the water gurgling and lapping by was so soothing that I began to doze.

I was recalled to my senses by a smothered cry from Bill, and, running to him, I found him staring to port in an intense and uncomfortable fashion. At my approach, he took one hand from the wheel, and gripped my arm so tightly that I was like to have screamed with the pain of it.

"Jack," said he, in a shaky voice, "while you was away something popped its head up, and looked over the ship's side."

"You've been dreaming," said I, in a voice which was a very fair imitation of Bill's own.

"Dreaming," repeated Bill, "dreaming! Ah, look there!"

He pointed with outstretched finger, and my heart seemed to stop beating as I saw a man's head appear above the side. For a brief space it peered at us in silence, and then a dark figure sprang like a cat on to the deck, and stood crouching a short distance away.

A mist came before my eyes, and my tongue failed me, but Bill let off a roar, such as I have never heard before or since. It was answered from below, both aft and for'ard, and the men came running up on deck just as they left their beds.

"What's up?" shouted the skipper, glancing aloft.

For answer, Bill pointed to the intruder, and the men, who had just caught sight of him, came up and formed a compact knot by the wheel.

"Come over the side, it did," panted Bill, "come over like a ghost out of the sea."

The skipper took one of the small lamps from the binnacle, and, holding it aloft, walked boldly up to the cause of alarm. In the little patch of light we saw a ghastly black-bearded man, dripping with water, regarding us with unwinking eyes, which glowed red in the light of the lamp.

"Where did you come from?" asked the skipper.

The figure shook its head.

"Where did you come from?" he repeated, walking up, and laying his hand on the other's shoulder.

Then the intruder spoke, but in a strange fashion and in strange words. We leaned forward to listen, but, even when he repeated them, we could make nothing of them.

"He's a furriner," said Roberts.

"Blest if I've ever 'eard the lingo afore," said Bill. "Does anybody rekernize it?"

Nobody did, and the skipper, after another attempt, gave it up, and, falling back upon the universal language of signs, pointed first to the man and then to the sea. The other understood him, and, in a heavy, slovenly fashion, portrayed a man drifting in an open boat, and clutching and clambering up the side of a passing ship. As his meaning dawned upon us, we rushed to the stern, and, leaning over, peered into the gloom, but the night was dark, and we saw nothing.

"Well," said the skipper, turning to Bill, with a mighty yawn, "take him below, and give him some grub, and the next time a gentleman calls on you, don't make such a confounded row about it."

He went below, followed by the mate, and after some slight hesitation, Roberts stepped up to the intruder, and signed to him to follow. He came stolidly enough, leaving a trail of water on the deck, and, after changing into the dry things we gave him, fell to, but without much appearance of hunger, upon some salt beef and biscuits, regarding us between bites with black, lack-lustre eyes.

"He seems as though he's a-walking in his sleep," said the cook.

"He ain't very hungry," said one of the men; "he seems to mumble his food."

"Hungry!" repeated Bill, who had just left the wheel. "Course he ain't famished. He had his tea last night."

The men stared at him in bewilderment.

"Don't you see?" said Bill, still in a hoarse whisper; "ain't you ever seen them eyes afore? Don't you know what he used to say about dying? It's Jem Dadd come back to us. Jem Dadd got another man's body, as he always said he would."

"Rot!" said Roberts, trying to speak bravely, but he got up, and, with the others, huddled together at the end of the fo'c's'le, and stared in a bewildered fashion at the sodden face and short, squat figure of our visitor. For his part, having finished his meal, he pushed his plate from him, and, leaning back on the locker, looked at the empty bunks.

Roberts caught his eye, and, with a nod and a wave of his hand, indicated the bunks. The fellow rose from the locker, and, amid a breathless silence, climbed into one of them—Jem Dadd's!

He slept in the dead sailor's bed that night, the only man in the fo'c's'le who did sleep properly, and turned out heavily and lumpishly in the morning for breakfast.

The skipper had him on deck after the meal, but could make nothing of him. To all his questions he replied in the strange tongue of the night before, and, though our fellows had been to many ports, and knew a word or two of several languages, none of them recognized it. The skipper gave it up at last, and, left to himself, he stared about him for some time, regardless of our interest in his movements, and then, leaning heavily against the side of the ship, stayed there so long that we thought he must have fallen asleep.

"He's half-dead now!" whispered Roberts.

"Hush!" said Bill, "mebbe he's been in the water a week or two, and can't quite make it out. See how he's looking at it now."

He stayed on deck all day in the sun, but, as night came on, returned to the warmth of the fo'c's'le. The food we gave him remained untouched, and he took little or no notice of us, though I fancied that he saw the fear we had of him. He slept again in the dead man's bunk, and when morning came still lay there.

Until dinner-time, nobody interfered with him, and then Roberts, pushed forward by the others, approached him with some food. He motioned, it away with a dirty, bloated hand, and, making signs for water, drank it eagerly.

For two days he stayed there quietly, the black eyes always open, the stubby fingers always on the move. On the third morning Bill, who had conquered his fear sufficiently to give him water occasionally, called softly to us.

"Come and look at him," said he. "What's the matter with him?"

"He's dying!" said the cook, with a shudder.

"He can't be going to die yet!" said Bill, blankly.

As he spoke the man's eyes seemed to get softer and more life-like, and he looked at us piteously and helplessly. From face to face he gazed in mute inquiry, and then, striking his chest feebly with his fist, uttered two words.

We looked at each other blankly, and he repeated them eagerly, and again touched his chest.

"It's his name," said the cook, and we all repeated them.

He smiled in an exhausted fashion, and then, rallying his energies, held up a forefinger; as we stared at this new riddle, he lowered it, and held up all four fingers, doubled.

"Come away," quavered the cook; "he's putting a spell on us."

We drew back at that, and back farther still, as he repeated the motions. Then Bill's face cleared suddenly, and he stepped towards him.

"He means his wife and younkers!" he shouted eagerly. "This ain't no Jem Dadd!"

It was good then to see how our fellows drew round the dying sailor, and strove to cheer him. Bill, to show he understood the finger business, nodded cheerily, and held his hand at four different heights from the floor. The last was very low, so low that the man set his lips together, and strove to turn his heavy head from us.

"Poor devil!" said Bill, "he wants us to tell his wife and children what's become of him. He must ha' been dying when he come aboard. What was his name, again?"

But the name was not easy to English lips, and we had already forgotten it.

"Ask him again," said the cook, "and write it down. Who's got a pen?"

He went to look for one as Bill turned to the sailor to get him to repeat it. Then he turned round again, and eyed us blankly, for, by this time, the owner had himself forgotten it.

PAYING OFF

My biggest fault, said the night-watchman, gloomily, has been good nature. I've spent the best part of my life trying to do my fellow-creeturs a good turn. And what do I get for it? If all the people I've helped was to come 'ere now there wouldn't be standing room for them on this wharf. 'Arf of them would be pushed overboard—and a good place for 'em, too.

I've been like it all my life. I was good-natured enough to go to sea as a boy because a skipper took a fancy to me and wanted my 'elp, and when I got older I was good-natured enough to get married. All my life I've given 'elp and advice free, and only a day or two ago one of 'em wot I 'ad given it to came round here with her 'usband and 'er two brothers and 'er mother and two or three people from the same street, to see her give me "wot for."

Another fault o' mine has been being sharp. Most people make mistakes, and they can't bear to see anybody as don't. Over and over agin I have showed people 'ow silly they 'ave been to do certain things, and told 'em wot I should ha' done in their place, but I can't remember one that ever gave me a "thank you" for it.

There was a man 'ere 'arf an hour ago that reminded me of both of these faults. He came in a-purpose to remind me, and 'e brought a couple o' grinning, brass-faced monkeys with 'im to see 'im do it. I was sitting on that barrel when he came, and arter two minutes I felt as if I was sitting on red-'ot cinders. He purtended he 'ad come in for the sake of old times and to ask arter my 'ealth, and all the time he was doing 'is best to upset me to amuse them two pore objecks 'e 'ad brought with 'im.

Capt'in Mellun is his name, and 'e was always a foolish, soft-'eaded sort o' man, and how he 'as kept 'is job I can't think. He used to trade between this wharf and Bristol on a little schooner called the *Firefly*, and seeing wot a silly, foolish kind o' man he was, I took a little bit o' notice of 'im. Many and many a time when 'e was going to do something he'd ha' been sorry for arterwards I 'ave taken 'im round to the Bear's Head and stood 'im pint arter pint until he began to see reason and own up that I was in the right.

His crew was a'most as bad as wot he was, and all in one month one o' the 'ands gave a man ten shillings for a di'mond ring he saw 'im pick up, wot turned out to be worth fourpence, and another one gave five bob for a meerschaum pipe made o' chalk. When I pointed out to 'em wot fools they was they didn't like it, and a week arterwards, when the skipper gave a man in a pub 'is watch and chain and two pounds to hold, to show 'is confidence in 'im, and I told 'im exactly wot I thought of him, 'e didn't like it.

"You're too sharp, Bill," he says, sneering like. "My opinion is that the pore man was run over. He told me 'e should only be away five minutes. And he 'ad got an honest face: nice open blue eyes, and a smile that done you good to look at."

"You've been swindled," I ses, "and you know it. If I'd been done like that I should never hold up my 'ead agin. Why, a child o' five would know better. You and your crew all seem to be tarred with the same brush. You ain't fit to be trusted out alone."

I believe 'e told his 'ands wot I said; anyway, two bits o' coke missed me by 'arf an inch next evening, and for some weeks not one of 'em spoke a word to me. When they see me coming they just used to stand up straight and twist their nose.

It didn't 'urt me, o' course. I took no notice of 'em. Even when one of 'em fell over the broom I was sweeping with I took no notice of 'im. I just went on with my work as if 'e wasn't there.

I suppose they 'ad been in the sulks about a month, and I was sitting 'ere one evening getting my breath arter a couple o' hours' 'ard work, when one of 'em, George Tebb by name, came off the ship and nodded to me as he passed.

"Evening, Bill," he ses.

"Evening," I ses, rather stiff.

"I wanted a word with you, Bill," he ses, in a low voice. "In fact, I might go so far as to say I want to ask you to do me a favour."

I looked at him so 'ard that he coughed and looked away.

"We might talk about it over a 'arf-pint," he ses.

"No, thank you," I ses. "I 'ad a 'arf-pint the day before yesterday, and I'm not thirsty."

He stood there fidgeting about for a bit, and then he puts his 'and on my shoulder.

"Well, come to the end of the jetty," he ses. "I've got something private to say."

I got up slow-like and followed 'im. I wasn't a bit curious. Not a bit. But if a man asks for my 'elp I always give it.

"It's like this," he ses, looking round careful, "only I don't want the other chaps to hear because I don't want to be laughed at. Last week an old uncle o' mine died and left me thirty pounds. It's just a week ago, and I've already got through five of 'em, and besides that the number of chaps that want to borrow ten bob for a couple o' days would surprise you."

"I ain't so easy surprised," I ses, shaking my 'ead.

"It ain't safe with me," he ses; "and the favour I want you to do is to take care of it for me. I know it'll go if I keep it. I've got it locked up in this box. And if you keep the box I'll keep the key, and when I want a bit I'll come and see you about it."

He pulled a little box out of 'is pocket and rattled it in my ear.

"There's five-and-twenty golden goblins in there," he ses. "If you take charge of 'em they'll be all right. If you don't, I'm pretty certain I sha'n't 'ave one of 'em in a week or two's time."

At fust I said I wouldn't 'ave anything to do with it, but he begged so 'ard that I began to alter my mind.

"You're as honest as daylight, Bill," he ses, very earnest. "I don't know another man in the world I could trust with twenty-five quid— especially myself. Now, put it in your pocket and look arter it for me. One of the quids in it is for you, for your trouble."

He slipped the box in my coat-pocket, and then he said 'is mind was so relieved that 'e felt like 'arf a pint. I was for going to the Bear's Head, the place I generally go to, because it is next door to the wharf, so to speak, but George wanted me to try the beer at another place he knew of.

"The wharf's all right," he ses. "There's one or two 'ands on the ship, and they won't let anybody run away with it."

From wot he said I thought the pub was quite close, but instead o' that I should think we walked pretty nearly a mile afore we got there. Nice snug place it was, and the beer was all right, although, as I told George Tebb, it didn't seem to me any better than the stuff at the Bear's Head.

He stood me two 'arf-pints and was just going to order another, when 'e found 'e 'adn't got any money left, and he wouldn't hear of me paying for it, because 'e said it was his treat.

"We'll 'ave a quid out o' the box," he ses. "I must 'ave one to go on with, anyway." I shook my 'ead at 'im.

"Only one," he ses, "and that'll last me a fortnight. Besides, I want to give you the quid I promised you."

I gave way at last, and he put his 'and in 'is trouser-pocket for the key, and then found it wasn't there.

"I must ha' left it in my chest," he ses. "I'll 'op back and get it." And afore I could prevent 'im he 'ad waved his 'and at me and gorn.

My fust idea was to go arter 'im, but I knew I couldn't catch 'im, and if I tried to meet 'im coming back I should most likely miss 'im through the side streets. So I sat there with my pipe and waited.

I suppose I 'ad been sitting down waiting for him for about ten minutes, when a couple o' sailormen came into the bar and began to make themselves a nuisance. Big fat chaps they was, and both of 'em more than 'arf sprung. And arter calling for a pint apiece they began to take a little notice of me.

"Where d'you come from?" ses one of 'em. "'Ome," I ses, very quiet.

"It's a good place—'ome," ses the chap, shaking his 'ead. "Can you sing "Ome, Sweet 'Ome'? You seem to 'ave got wot I might call a 'singing face.'"

"Never mind about my face," I ses, very sharp. "You mind wot you're doing with that beer. You'll 'ave it over in a minute."

The words was 'ardly out of my mouth afore 'e gave a lurch and spilt his pint all over me. From 'ead to foot I was dripping with beer, and I was in such a temper I wonder I didn't murder 'im; but afore I could move they both pulled out their pocket-'ankerchers and started to rub me down.

"That'll do," I ses at last, arter they 'ad walked round me 'arf-a-dozen times and patted me all over to see if I was dry. "You get off while you're safe."

"It was my mistake, mate," ses the chap who 'ad spilt the beer.

"You get outside," I ses. "Go on, both of you, afore I put you out."

They gave one look at me, standing there with my fists clenched, and then they went out like lambs, and I 'eard 'em trot round the corner as though they was afraid I was following. I felt a little bit damp and chilly, but beer is like sea-water—you don't catch cold through it—and I sat down agin to wait for George Tebb.

He came in smiling and out 'o breath in about ten minutes' time, with the key in 'is 'and, and as soon as I told 'im wot had 'appened to me with the beer he turned to the landlord and ordered me six o' rum 'ot at once.

"Drink that up," he ses, 'anding it to me; "but fust of all give me the box, so as I can pay for it."

I put my 'and in my pocket. Then I put it in the other one, and arter that I stood staring at George Tebb and shaking all over.

"Wot's the matter? Wot are you looking like that for?" he ses.

"It must ha' been them two," I ses, choking. "While they was purtending to dry me and patting me all over they must 'ave taken it out of my pocket."

"Wot are you talking about?" ses George, staring at me.

"The box 'as gorn," I ses, putting down the 'ot rum and feeling in my trouser-pocket. "The box 'as gorn, and them two must 'ave taken it."

"Gorn!" ses George. "Gorn! My box with twenty-five pounds in, wot I trusted you with, gorn? Wot are you talking about? It can't be—it's too crool!"

He made such a noise that the landlord wot was waiting for 'is money, asked 'im wot he meant by it, and, arter he 'ad explained, I'm blest if the landlord didn't advise him to search me. I stood still and let George go through my pockets, and then I told 'im I 'ad done with 'im and I never wanted to see 'im agin as long as I lived.

"I dare say," ses George, "I dare say. But you'll come along with me to the wharf and see the skipper. I'm not going to lose five-and-twenty quid through your carelessness."

I marched along in front of 'im with my 'ead in the air, and when he spoke to me I didn't answer him. He went aboard the ship when we got to the wharf, and a minute or two arterwards 'e came to the side and said the skipper wanted to see me.

The airs the skipper gave 'imself was sickening. He sat down there in 'is miserable little rat-'ole of a cabin and acted as if 'e was a judge and I was a prisoner. Most of the 'ands 'ad squeezed in there too, and the things they advised George to do to me was remarkable.

"Silence!" ses the skipper. "Now, watchman, tell me exactly 'ow this thing 'appened."

"I've told you once," I ses.

"I know," ses the skipper, "but I want you to tell me again to see if you contradict yourself. I can't understand 'ow such a clever man as you could be done so easy."

I thought I should ha' bust, but I kept my face wonderful. I just asked 'im wot the men was like that got off with 'is watch and chain and two pounds, in case they might be the same.

"That's different," he ses.

"Oh!" ses I. "'Ow?"

"I lost my own property," he ses, "but you lost George's, and 'ow a man like you, that's so much sharper and cleverer than other people, could be had so easy, I can't think. Why, a child of five would ha' known better."

"A baby in arms would ha' known better," ses the man wot 'ad bought the di'mond ring. "'Ow could you 'ave been so silly, Bill? At your time o' life, too!"

"That's neither 'ere nor there," ses the skip-per. "The watchman has lost twenty-five quid belonging to one o' my men. The question is, wot is he going to do about it?"

"Nothing," I ses. "I didn't ask 'im to let me mind the box. He done it of 'is own free will. It's got nothing to do with me."

"Oh, hasn't it?" ses the skipper, drawing 'imself up. "I don't want to be too 'ard on you, but at the same time I can't let my man suffer. I'll make it as easy as I can, and I order you to pay 'im five shillings a week till the twenty-five pounds is cleared off."

I laughed; I couldn't 'elp it. I just stood there and laughed at 'im.

"If you don't," ses the skipper, "then I shall lay the facts of the case afore the guv'nor. Whether he'll object to you being in a pub a mile away, taking care of a box of gold while you was supposed to be taking care of the wharf, is his bisness. My bisness is to see that my man 'as 'is rights."

"'Ear, 'ear !" ses the crew.

"You please yourself, watchman," ses the skipper. "You're such a clever man that no doubt you could get a better job to-morrow. There must be 'eaps of people wanting a man like you. It's for you to decide. That's all I've got to say—five bob a week till pore George 'as got 'is money back, or else I put the case afore the guv'nor. Wot did you say?"

I said it agin, and, as 'e didn't seem to understand, I said it once more.

"Please yourself," 'e ses, when I 'ad finished. "You're an old man, and five bob a week can't be much loss to you. You've got nothing to spend it on, at your time o' life. And you've got a very soft job 'ere. Wot?"

I didn't answer 'im. I just turned round, and, arter giving a man wot stood in my way a punch in the chest, I got up on deck and on to the wharf, and said my little say all alone to myself, behind the crane.

I paid the fust five bob to George Tebb the next time the ship was up, and arter biting 'em over and over agin and then ringing 'em on the deck 'e took the other chaps round to the Bear's Head.

"P'r'aps it's just as well it's 'appened," he ses. "Five bob a week for nearly two years ain't to be sneezed at. It's slow, but it's sure."

I thought 'e was joking at fust, but arter working it out in the office with a bit o' pencil and paper I thought I should ha' gorn crazy. And when I complained about the time to George 'e said I could make it shorter if I liked by paying ten bob a week, but 'e thought the steady five bob a week was best for both of us.

I got to 'ate the sight of 'im. Every week regular as clockwork he used to come round to me with his 'and out, and then go and treat 'is mates to beer with my money. If the ship came up in the day-time, at six o'clock in the evening he'd be at the wharf gate waiting for me; and if it came up at night she was no sooner made fast than 'e was over the side patting my trouser-pocket and saying wot a good job it was for both of us that I was in steady employment.

Week arter week and month arter month I went on paying. I a'most forgot the taste o' beer, and if I could manage to get a screw o' baccy a week I thought myself lucky. And at last, just as I thought I couldn't stand it any longer, the end came.

I 'ad just given George 'is week's money—and 'ow I got it together that week I don't know—when one o' the chaps came up and said the skipper wanted to see me on board at once.

"Tell 'im if he wants to see me I'm to be found on the wharf," I ses, very sharp.

"He wants to see you about George's money," ses the chap. "I should go if I was you. My opinion is he wants to do you a good turn."

I 'ung fire for a bit, and then, arter sweeping up for a little while deliberate-like, I put down my broom and stepped aboard to see the skipper, wot was sitting on the cabin skylight purtending to read a newspaper.

He put it down when 'e see me, and George and the others, wot 'ad been standing in a little bunch for'ard, came aft and stood looking on.

"I wanted to see you about this money, watchman," ses the skipper, putting on 'is beastly frills agin. "O' course, we all feel that to a pore man like you it's a bit of a strain, and, as George ses, arter all you have been more foolish than wicked."

"Much more," ses George.

"I find that you 'ave now paid five bob a week for nineteen weeks," ses the skipper, "and George 'as been kind enough and generous enough to let you off the rest. There's no need for you to look bashful, George; it's a credit to you."

I could 'ardly believe my ears. George stood there grinning like a stuck fool, and two o' the chaps was on their best behaviour with their 'ands over their mouths and their eyes sticking out.

"That's all, watchman," ses the skipper; "and I 'ope it'll be a lesson to you not to neglect your dooty by going into public-'ouses and taking charge of other people's money when you ain't fit for it."

"I sha'n't try to do anybody else a kindness agin, if that's wot you mean," I ses, looking at 'im.

"No, you'd better not," he ses. "This partickler bit o' kindness 'as cost you four pounds fifteen, and that's a curious thing when you come to think of it. Very curious."

"Wot d'ye mean?" I ses.

"Why," he ses, grinning like a madman, "it's just wot we lost between us. I lost a watch and chain worth two pounds, and another couple o' pounds besides; Joe lost ten shillings over 'is di'mond ring; and Charlie lost five bob over a pipe. 'That's four pounds fifteen—just the same as you."

Them silly fools stood there choking and sobbing and patting each other on the back as though they'd never leave off, and all of a sudden I 'ad a 'orrible suspicion that I 'ad been done.

"Did you see the sovereigns in the box?" I ses, turning to the skipper.

"No," he ses, shaking his 'ead.

"'Ow do you know they was there, then?" ses I.

"Because you took charge of 'em," said the skipper; "and I know wot a clever, sharp chap you are. It stands to reason that you wouldn't be responsible for a box like that unless you saw inside of it. Why, a child o' five wouldn't!"

I stood there looking at 'im, but he couldn't meet my eye. None of 'em could; and arter waiting there for a minute or two to give 'em a chance, I turned my back on 'em and went off to my dooty.

The old man sat on his accustomed bench outside the Cauliflower. A generous measure of beer stood in a blue and white jug by his elbow, and little wisps of smoke curled slowly upward from the bowl of his churchwarden pipe. The knapsacks of two young men lay where they were flung on the table, and the owners, taking a noon-tide rest, turned a polite, if bored, ear to the reminiscences of grateful old age.

Poaching, said the old man, who had tried topics ranging from early turnips to horseshoeing—poaching ain't wot it used to be in these 'ere parts. Nothing is like it used to be, poaching nor anything else; but that there man you might ha' noticed as went out about ten minutes ago and called me "Old Truthfulness" as 'e passed is the worst one I know. Bob Pretty 'is name is, and of all the sly, artful, deceiving men that ever lived in Claybury 'e is the worst—never did a honest day's work in 'is life and never wanted the price of a glass of ale.

Bob Pretty's worst time was just after old Squire Brown died. The old squire couldn't afford to preserve much, but by-and-by a gentleman with plenty o' money, from London, named Rockett, took 'is place and things began to look up. Pheasants was 'is favourites, and 'e spent no end o' money rearing of 'em, but anything that could be shot at suited 'im, too.

He started by sneering at the little game that Squire Brown 'ad left, but all 'e could do didn't seem to make much difference; things disappeared in a most eggstrordinary way, and the keepers went pretty near crazy, while the things the squire said about Claybury and Claybury men was disgraceful.

Everybody knew as it was Bob Pretty and one or two of 'is mates from other places, but they couldn't prove it. They couldn't catch 'im nohow, and at last the squire 'ad two keepers set off to watch 'im by night and by day.

Bob Pretty wouldn't believe it; he said 'e couldn't. And even when it was pointed out to 'im that Keeper Lewis was follering of 'im he said that it just 'appened he was going the same way, that was all. And sometimes 'e'd get up in the middle of the night and go for a fifteen-mile walk 'cos 'e'd got the toothache, and Mr. Lewis, who 'adn't got it, had to tag along arter 'im till he was fit to drop. O' course, it was one keeper the less to look arter the game, and by-and-by the squire see that and took 'im off.

All the same they kept a pretty close watch on Bob, and at last one arternoon they sprang out on 'im as he was walking past Gray's farm, and asked him wot it was he 'ad in his pockets.

"That's my bisness, Mr. Lewis," ses Bob Pretty.

Mr. Smith, the other keeper, passed 'is hands over Bob's coat and felt something soft and bulgy.

"You take your 'ands off of me," ses Bob; "you don't know 'ow partikler I am."

He jerked 'imself away, but they caught 'old of 'im agin, and Mr. Lewis put 'is hand in his inside pocket and pulled out two brace o' partridges.

"You'll come along of us," he ses, catching 'im by the arm.

"We've been looking for you a long time," ses Keeper Smith, "and it's a pleasure for us to 'ave your company."

Bob Pretty said 'e wouldn't go, but they forced 'im along and took 'im all the way to Cudford, four miles off, so that Policeman White could lock 'im up for the night. Mr. White was a'most as pleased as the keepers, and 'e warned Bob solemn not to speak becos all 'e said would be used agin 'im.

"Never mind about that," ses Bob Pretty. "I've got a clear conscience, and talking can't 'urt me. I'm very glad to see you, Mr. White; if these two clever, experienced keepers hadn't brought me I should 'ave looked you up myself. They've been and stole my partridges."

Them as was standing round laughed, and even Policeman White couldn't 'elp giving a little smile.

"There's nothing to laugh at," ses Bob, 'olding his 'ead up. "It's a fine thing when a working man—a 'ardworking man—can't take home a little game for 'is family without being stopped and robbed."

"I s'pose they flew into your pocket?" ses Police-man White.

"No, they didn't," ses Bob. "I'm not going to tell any lies about it; I put 'em there. The partridges in my inside coat-pocket and the bill in my waistcoat-pocket."

"The bill?" ses Keeper Lewis, staring at 'im.

"Yes, the bill," ses Bob Pretty, staring back at 'im; "the bill from Mr. Keen, the poulterer, at Wick-ham."

He fetched it out of 'is pocket and showed it to Mr. White, and the keepers was like madmen a'most 'cos it was plain to see that Bob Pretty 'ad been and bought them partridges just for to play a game on 'em.

"I was curious to know wot they tasted like," he ses to the policeman. "Worst of it is, I don't s'pose my pore wife'll know 'ow to cook 'em."

"You get off 'ome," ses Policeman White, staring at 'im.

"But ain't I goin' to be locked up?" ses Bob. "'Ave I been brought all this way just to 'ave a little chat with a policeman I don't like."

"You go 'ome," ses Policeman White, handing the partridges back to 'im.

"All right," ses Bob, "and I may 'ave to call you to witness that these 'ere two men laid hold o' me and tried to steal my partridges. I shall go up and see my loryer about it."

He walked off 'ome with his 'ead up as high as 'e could hold it, and the airs 'e used to give 'imself arter this was terrible for to behold. He got 'is eldest boy to write a long letter to the squire about it, saying that 'e'd overlook it this time, but 'e couldn't promise for the future. Wot with Bob Pretty on one side and Squire Rockett on the other, them two keepers' lives was 'ardly worth living.

Then the squire got a head-keeper named Cutts, a man as was said to know more about the ways of poachers than they did themselves. He was said to 'ave cleared out all the poachers for miles round the place 'e came from, and pheasants could walk into people's cottages and not be touched.

He was a sharp-looking man, tall and thin, with screwed-up eyes and a little red beard. The second day 'e came 'e was up here at this 'ere Cauliflower, having a pint o' beer and looking round at the chaps as he talked to the landlord. The odd thing was that men who'd never taken a hare or a pheasant in their lives could 'ardly meet 'is eye, while Bob Pretty stared at 'im as if 'e was a wax-works.

"I 'ear you 'ad a little poaching in these parts afore I came," ses Mr. Cutts to the landlord.

"I think I 'ave 'eard something o' the kind," ses the landlord, staring over his 'ead with a far-away look in 'is eyes.

"You won't hear of much more," ses the keeper. "I've invented a new way of catching the dirty rascals; afore I came 'ere I caught all the poachers on three estates. I clear 'em out just like a ferret clears out rats."

"Sort o' man-trap?" ses the landlord.

"Ah, that's tellings," ses Mr. Cutts.

"Well, I 'ope you'll catch 'em here," ses Bob Pretty; "there's far too many of 'em about for my liking. Far too many."

"I shall 'ave 'em afore long," ses Mr. Cutts, nodding his 'ead.

"Your good 'ealth," ses Bob Pretty, holding up 'is mug. "We've been wanting a man like you for a long time."

"I don't want any of your impidence, my man," ses the keeper. "I've 'eard about you, and nothing good either. You be careful."

"I am careful," ses Bob, winking at the others. "I 'ope you'll catch all them low poaching chaps; they give the place a bad name, and I'm a'most afraid to go out arter dark for fear of meeting 'em."

Peter Gubbins and Sam Jones began to laugh, but Bob Pretty got angry with 'em and said he didn't see there was anything to laugh at. He said that poaching was a disgrace to their native place, and instead o' laughing they ought to be thankful to Mr. Cutts for coming to do away with it all.

"Any help I can give you shall be given cheerful," he ses to the keeper.

"When I want your help I'll ask you for it," ses Mr. Cutts.

"Thankee," ses Bob Pretty. "I on'y 'ope I sha'n't get my face knocked about like yours 'as been, that's all; 'cos my wife's so partikler."

"Wot d'ye mean?" ses Mr. Cutts, turning on him. "My face ain't been knocked about."

"Oh, I beg your pardin," ses Bob; "I didn't know it was natural."

Mr. Cutts went black in the face a'most and stared at Bob Pretty as if 'e was going to eat 'im, and Bob stared back, looking fust at the keeper's nose and then at 'is eyes and mouth, and then at 'is nose agin.

"You'll know me agin, I s'pose?" ses Mr. Cutts, at last.

"Yes," ses Bob, smiling; "I should know you a mile off—on the darkest night."

"We shall see," ses Mr. Cutts, taking up 'is beer and turning 'is back on him. "Those of us as live the longest'll see the most."

"I'm glad I've lived long enough to see 'im," ses Bob to Bill Chambers. "I feel more satisfied with myself now."

Bill Chambers coughed, and Mr. Cutts, arter finishing 'is beer, took another look at Bob Pretty, and went off boiling a'most.

The trouble he took to catch Bob Pretty arter that you wouldn't believe, and all the time the game seemed to be simply melting away, and Squire Rockett was finding fault with 'im all day long. He was worn to a shadder a'most with watching, and Bob Pretty seemed to be more prosperous than ever.

Sometimes Mr. Cutts watched in the plantations, and sometimes 'e hid 'imself near Bob's house, and at last one night, when 'e was crouching behind the fence of Frederick Scott's front garden, 'e saw Bob Pretty come out of 'is house and, arter a careful look round, walk up the road. He held 'is breath as Bob passed 'im, and was just getting up to foller 'im when Bob stopped and walked slowly back agin, sniffing.

"Wot a delicious smell o' roses!" he ses, out loud.

He stood in the middle o' the road nearly opposite where the keeper was hiding, and sniffed so that you could ha' 'eard him the other end o' the village.

"It can't be roses," he ses, in a puzzled voice, "be-cos there ain't no roses hereabouts, and, besides, it's late for 'em. It must be Mr. Cutts, the clever new keeper."

He put his 'ead over the fence and bid 'im good evening, and said wot a fine night for a stroll it was, and asked 'im whether 'e was waiting for Frederick Scott's aunt. Mr. Cutts didn't answer 'im a word; 'e was pretty near bursting with passion. He got up and shook 'is fist in Bob Pretty's face, and then 'e went off stamping down the road as if 'e was going mad.

And for a time Bob Pretty seemed to 'ave all the luck on 'is side. Keeper Lewis got rheumatic fever, which 'e put down to sitting about night arter night in damp places watching for Bob, and, while 'e was in the thick of it, with the doctor going every day, Mr. Cutts fell in getting over a fence and broke 'is leg. Then all the work fell on Keeper Smith, and to 'ear 'im talk you'd think that rheumatic fever and broken legs was better than anything else in the world. He asked the squire for 'elp, but the squire wouldn't give it to 'im, and he kept telling 'im wot a feather in 'is cap it would be if 'e did wot the other two couldn't do, and caught Bob Pretty. It was all very well, but, as Smith said, wot 'e wanted was feathers in 'is piller, instead of 'aving to snatch a bit o' sleep in 'is chair or sitting down with his 'ead agin a tree. When I tell you that 'e fell asleep in this public-'ouse one night while the landlord was drawing a pint o' beer he 'ad ordered, you'll know wot 'e suffered.

O' course, all this suited Bob Pretty as well as could be, and 'e was that good-tempered 'e'd got a nice word for everybody, and when Bill Chambers told 'im 'e was foolhardy 'e only laughed and said 'e knew wot 'e was about.

But the very next night 'e had reason to remember Bill Chambers's words. He was walking along Farmer Hall's field—the one next to the squire's plantation—and, so far from being nervous, 'e was actually a-whistling. He'd got a sack over 'is shoulder, loaded as full as it could be, and 'e 'ad just stopped to light 'is pipe when three men burst out o' the plantation and ran toward 'im as 'ard as they could run.

Bob Pretty just gave one look and then 'e dropped 'is pipe and set off like a hare. It was no good dropping the sack, because Smith, the keeper, 'ad recognised 'im and called 'im by name, so 'e just put 'is teeth together and did the best he could, and there's no doubt that if it 'adn't ha' been for the sack 'e could 'ave got clear away.

As it was, 'e ran for pretty near a mile, and they could 'ear 'im breathing like a pair o' bellows; but at last 'e saw that the game was up. He just man-aged to struggle as far as Farmer Pinnock's pond, and then, waving the sack round his 'ead, 'e flung it into the middle of it, and fell down gasping for breath.

"Got—you—this time—Bob Pretty," ses one o' the men, as they came up.

"Wot—Mr. Cutts?" ses Bob, with a start. "That's me, my man," ses the keeper.

"Why—I thought—you was. Is that Mr. Lewis? It can't be."

"That's me," ses Keeper Lewis. "We both got well sudden-like, Bob Pretty, when we 'eard you was out. You ain't so sharp as you thought you was."

Bob Pretty sat still, getting 'is breath back and doing a bit o' thinking at the same time.

"You give me a start," he ses, at last. "I thought you was both in bed, and, knowing 'ow hard worked Mr. Smith 'as been, I just came round to 'elp 'im keep watch like. I promised to 'elp you, Mr. Cutts, if you remember."

"Wot was that you threw in the pond just now?" ses Mr. Cutts.

"A sack," ses Bob Pretty; "a sack I found in Farmer Hall's field. It felt to me as though it might 'ave birds in it, so I picked it up, and I was just on my way to your 'ouse with it, Mr. Cutts, when you started arter me."

"Ah!" ses the keeper, "and wot did you run for?"

Bob Pretty tried to laugh. "Becos I thought it was the poachers arter me," he ses. "It seems ridikilous, don't it?"

"Yes, it does," ses Lewis.

"I thought you'd know me a mile off," ses Mr. Cutts. "I should ha' thought the smell o' roses would ha' told you I was near."

Bob Pretty scratched 'is 'ead and looked at 'im out of the corner of 'is eye, but he 'adn't got any answer. Then 'e sat biting his finger-nails and thinking while the keepers stood argyfying as to who should take 'is clothes off and go into the pond arter the pheasants. It was a very cold night and the pond was pretty deep in places, and none of 'em seemed anxious.

"Make 'im go in for it," ses Lewis, looking at Bob; "'e chucked it in."

"On'y Becos I thought you was poachers," ses Bob. "I'm sorry to 'ave caused so much trouble."

"Well, you go in and get it out," ses Lewis, who pretty well guessed who'd 'ave to do it if Bob didn't. "It'll look better for you, too."

"I've got my defence all right," ses Bob Pretty. "I ain't set a foot on the squire's preserves, and I found this sack a 'undred yards away from it."

"Don't waste more time," ses Mr. Cutts to Lewis.

"Off with your clothes and in with you. Anybody'd think you was afraid of a little cold water."

"Whereabouts did 'e pitch it in?" ses Lewis.

Bob Pretty pointed with 'is finger exactly where 'e thought it was, but they wouldn't listen to 'im, and then Lewis, arter twice saying wot a bad cold he'd got, took 'is coat off very slow and careful.

"I wouldn't mind going in to oblige you," ses Bob Pretty, "but the pond is so full o' them cold, slimy efts; I don't fancy them crawling up agin me, and, besides that, there's such a lot o' deep holes in it. And wotever you do don't put your 'ead under; you know 'ow foul that water is."

Keeper Lewis pretended not to listen to 'im. He took off 'is clothes very slowly and then 'e put one foot in and stood shivering, although Smith, who felt the water with his 'and, said it was quite warm. Then Lewis put the other foot in and began to walk about careful, 'arf-way up to 'is knees.

"I can't find it," he ses, with 'is teeth chattering.

"You 'aven't looked," ses Mr. Cutts; "walk about more; you can't expect to find it all at once. Try the middle."

Lewis tried the middle, and 'e stood there up to 'is neck, feeling about with his foot and saying things out loud about Bob Pretty, and other things under 'is breath about Mr. Cutts.

"Well, I'm going off 'ome," ses Bob Pretty, getting up. "I'm too tender-'arted to stop and see a man drownded."

"You stay 'ere," ses Mr. Cutts, catching 'old of him.

"Wot for?" ses Bob; "you've got no right to keep me 'ere."

"Catch 'old of 'im, Joe," ses Mr. Cutts, quick-like.

Smith caught 'old of his other arm, and Lewis left off trying to find the sack to watch the struggle. Bob Pretty fought 'ard, and once or twice 'e nearly tumbled Mr. Cutts into the pond, but at last 'e gave in and lay down panting and talking about 'is loryer. Smith 'eld him down on the ground while Mr. Cutts kept pointing out places with 'is finger for Lewis to walk to. The last place 'e pointed to wanted a much taller man, but it wasn't found out till too late, and the fuss Keeper Lewis made when 'e could speak agin was terrible.

"You'd better come out," ses Mr. Cutts; "you ain't doing no good. We know where they are and we'll watch the pond till daylight—that is, unless Smith 'ud like to 'ave a try."

"It's pretty near daylight now, I think," ses Smith.

Lewis came out and ran up and down to dry 'imself, and finished off on 'is pocket-'andkerchief, and then with 'is teeth chattering 'e began to dress 'imself. He got 'is shirt on, and then 'e stood turning over 'is clothes as if 'e was looking for something.

"Never mind about your stud now," ses Mr. Cutts; "hurry up and dress."

"Stud?" ses Lewis, very snappish. "I'm looking for my trowsis."

"Your trowsis?" ses Smith, 'elping 'im look.

"I put all my clothes together," ses Lewis, a'most shouting. "Where are they? I'm 'arf perished with cold. Where are they?"

"He 'ad 'em on this evening," ses Bob Pretty, "'cos I remember noticing 'em."

"They must be somewhere about," ses Mr. Cutts; "why don't you use your eyes?"

He walked up and down, peering about, and as for Lewis he was 'opping round 'arf crazy.

"I wonder," ses Bob Pretty, in a thoughtful voice, to Smith—"I wonder whether you or Mr. Cutts kicked 'em in the pond while you was struggling with me. Come to think of it, I seem to remember 'earing a splash."

"He's done it, Mr. Cutts," ses Smith; "never mind, it'll go all the 'arder with 'im."

"But I do mind," ses Lewis, shouting. "I'll be even with you for this, Bob Pretty. I'll make you feel it. You wait till I've done with you. You'll get a month extra for this, you see if you don't."

"Don't you mind about me," ses Bob; "you run off 'ome and cover up them legs of yours. I found that sack, so my conscience is clear."

Lewis put on 'is coat and waistcoat and set off, and Mr. Cutts and Smith, arter feeling about for a dry place, set theirselves down and began to smoke.

"Look 'ere," ses Bob Pretty, "I'm not going to sit 'ere all night to please you; I'm going off 'ome. If you want me you'll know where to find me."

"You stay where you are," ses Mr. Cutts. "We ain't going to let you out of our sight."

"Very well, then, you take me 'ome," ses Bob. "I'm not going to catch my death o' cold sitting 'ere. I'm not used to being out of a night like you are. I was brought up respectable."

"I dare say," ses Mr. Cutts. "Take you 'ome, and then 'ave one o' your mates come and get the sack while we're away."

Then Bob Pretty lost 'is temper, and the things 'e said about Mr. Cutts wasn't fit for Smith to 'ear. He threw 'imself down at last full length on the ground and sulked till the day broke.

Keeper Lewis was there a'most as soon as it was light, with some long hay-rakes he'd borrowed, and I should think that pretty near 'arf the folks in Clay-bury 'ad turned up to see the fun. Mrs. Pretty was crying and wringing 'er 'ands; but most folks seemed to be rather pleased that Bob 'ad been caught at last.

In next to no time 'arf-a-dozen rakes was at work, and the things they brought out o' that pond you wouldn't believe. The edge of it was all littered with rusty tin pails and saucepans and such-like, and by-and-by Lewis found the things he'd 'ad to go 'ome without a few hours afore, but they didn't seem to find that sack, and Bob Pretty, wot was talking to 'is wife, began to look 'opeful.

But just then the squire came riding up with two friends as was staying with 'im, and he offered a reward of five shillings to the man wot found it. Three or four of 'em waded in up to their middle then and raked their 'ardest, and at last Henery Walker give a cheer and brought it to the side, all heavy with water.

"That's the sack I found, sir," ses Bob, starting up. "It wasn't on your land at all, but on the field next to it. I'm an honest, 'ardworking man, and I've never been in trouble afore. Ask anybody 'ere and they'll tell you the same."

Squire Rockett took no notice of 'im. "Is that the sack?" he asks, turning to Mr. Cutts.

"That's the one, sir," ses Mr. Cutts. "I'd swear to it anywhere."

"You'd swear a man's life away," ses Bob. "'Ow can you swear to it when it was dark?"

Mr. Cutts didn't answer 'im. He went down on 'is knees and cut the string that tied up the mouth o' the sack, and then 'e started back as if 'e'd been shot, and 'is eyes a'most started out of 'is 'ead.

"Wot's the matter?" ses the squire.

Mr. Cutts couldn't speak; he could only stutter and point at the sack with 'is finger, and Henery Walker, as was getting curious, lifted up the other end of it and out rolled a score of as fine cabbages as you could wish to see.

I never see people so astonished afore in all my born days, and as for Bob Pretty, 'e stood staring at them cabbages as if 'e couldn't believe 'is eyesight.

"And that's wot I've been kept 'ere all night for," he ses, at last, shaking his 'ead. "That's wot comes o' trying to do a kindness to keepers, and 'elping of 'em in their difficult work. P'r'aps that ain't the sack arter all, Mr. Cutts. I could ha' sworn they was pheasants in the one I found, but I may be mistook, never 'aving 'ad one in my 'ands afore. Or p'r'aps somebody was trying to 'ave a game with you, Mr. Cutts, and deceived me instead."

The keepers on'y stared at 'im.

"You ought to be more careful," ses Bob. "Very likely while you was taking all that trouble over me, and Keeper Lewis was catching 'is death o' cold, the poachers was up at the plantation taking all they wanted. And, besides, it ain't right for Squire Rockett to 'ave to pay Henery Walker five shillings for finding a lot of old cabbages. I shouldn't like it myself."

He looked out of the corner of 'is eye at the squire, as was pretending not to notice Henery Walker touching 'is cap to him, and then 'e turns to 'is wife and he ses:

"Come along, old gal," 'e ses. "I want my breakfast bad, and arter that I shall 'ave to lose a honest day's work in bed."

PETER'S PENCE

Sailormen don't bother much about their relations, as a rule, said the night-watchman; sometimes because a railway-ticket costs as much as a barrel o' beer, and they ain't got the money for both, and sometimes because most relations run away with the idea that a sailorman has been knocking about 'arf over the world just to bring them 'ome presents.

Then, agin, some relations are partikler about appearances, and they don't like it if a chap don't wear a collar and tidy 'imself up. Dress is everything nowadays; put me in a top 'at and a tail-coat, with a twopenny smoke stuck in my mouth, and who would know the difference between me and a lord? Put a bishop in my clothes, and you'd ask 'im to 'ave a 'arf-pint as soon as you would me— sooner, p'r'aps.

Talking of relations reminds me of Peter Russet's uncle. It's some years ago now, and Peter and old Sam Small and Ginger Dick 'ad just come back arter being away for nearly ten months. They 'ad all got money in their pockets, and they was just talking about the spree they was going to have, when a letter was brought to Peter, wot had been waiting for 'im at the office.

He didn't like opening it at fust. The last letter he had 'ad kept 'im hiding indoors for a week, and then made him ship a fortnight afore 'e had meant to. He stood turning it over and over, and at last, arter Sam, wot was always a curious man, 'ad told 'im that if he didn't open it he'd do it for 'im, he tore it open and read it.

"It's from my old uncle, George Goodman," he ses, staring. "Why, I ain't seen 'im for over twenty years."

"Do you owe 'im any money?" ses Sam.

Peter shook his 'ead. "He's up in London," he ses, looking at the letter agin, "up in London for the fust time in thirty-three years, and he wants to come and stay with me so that I can show 'im about."

"Wot is he?" ses Sam.

"He's retired," ses Peter, trying not to speak proud.

"Got money?" ses Sam, with a start.

"I b'leeve so," ses Peter, in a off-hand way. "I don't s'pose 'e lives on air."

"Any wives or children?" ses Sam.

"No," ses Peter. "He 'ad a wife, but she died."

"Then you have 'im, Peter," ses Sam, wot was always looking out for money. "Don't throw away a oppertunity like that. Why, if you treat 'im well he might leave it all to you."

"No such luck," ses Peter.

"You do as Sam ses," ses Ginger. "I wish I'd got an uncle."

"We'll try and give 'im a good time," ses Sam, "and if he's anything like Peter we shall enjoy ourselves."

"Yes; but he ain't," ses Peter. "He's a very solemn, serious-minded man, and a strong teetotaller. Wot you'd call a glass o' beer he'd call pison. That's 'ow he got on. He's thought a great deal of in 'is place, I can tell you, but he ain't my sort."

"That's a bit orkard," ses Sam, scratching his 'ead. "Same time, it don't do to throw away a chance. If 'e was my uncle I should pretend to be a teetotaller while 'e was here, just to please 'im."

"And when you felt like a drink, Peter," ses Ginger, "me and Sam would look arter 'im while you slipped off to get it."

"He could 'ave the room below us," ses Sam. "It is empty."

Peter gave a sniff. "Wot about you and Ginger?" he ses.

"Wot about us?" ses Sam and Ginger, both together.

"Why, you'd 'ave to be teetotallers, too," ses Peter. "Woes the good o' me pretending to be steady if 'e sees I've got pals like you?"

Sam scratched his 'ead agin, ever so long, and at last he ses, "Well, mate," he ses, "drink don't trouble me nor Ginger. We can do without it, as far as that goes; and we must all take it in turns to keep the old gentleman busy while the others go and get wot they want. You'd better go and take the room downstairs for 'im, afore it goes."

Peter looked at 'im in surprise, but that was Sam all over. The idea o' knowing a man with money was too much for 'im, and he sat there giving good advice to Peter about 'is behavior until Peter didn't know whether it was 'is uncle or Sam's. 'Owever, he took the room and wrote the letter, and next arternoon at three o'clock Mr. Goodman came in a four-wheel cab with a big bag and a fat umbrella. A short, stiffish-built man of about sixty he was, with 'is top lip shaved and a bit o' short gray beard. He 'ad on a top 'at and a tail-coat, black kid gloves and a little black bow, and he didn't answer the cabman back a single word.

He seemed quite pleased to see Peter, and by and by Sam, who was bursting with curiosity, came down-stairs to ask Peter to lend 'im a boot-lace, and was interduced. Then Ginger came down to look for Sam, and in a few minutes they was all talking as comfortable as possible.

"I ain't seen Peter for twenty years," ses Mr. Goodman—"twenty long years!"

Sam shook his 'ead and looked at the floor.

"I happened to go and see Peter's sister—my niece Polly," ses Mr. Goodman, "and she told me the name of 'is ship. It was quite by chance, because she told me it was the fust letter she had 'ad from him in seven years."

"I didn't think it was so long as that," ses Peter. "Time passes so quick."

His uncle nodded. "Ah, so it does," 'e ses. "It's all the same whether we spend it on the foaming ocean or pass our little lives ashore. Afore we can turn round, in a manner o' speaking, it 'as gorn."

"The main thing," ses Peter, in a good voice, "is to pass it properly."

"Then it don't matter," ses Ginger.

"So it don't," ses Sam, very serious.

"I held 'im in my arms when 'e was a baby," ses Mr. Goodman, looking at Peter.

"Fond o' children?" ses Sam.

Mr. Goodman nodded. "Fond of everybody," he ses.

"That's 'ow Peter is," ses Ginger; "specially young—"

Peter Russet and Sam both turned and looked at 'im very sharp.

"Children," ses Ginger, remembering 'imself, "*and* teetotallers. I s'pose it is being a teetotaller 'imself."

"Is Peter a teetotaller?" ses Mr. Goodman. "I'd no idea of it. Wot a joyful thing!"

"It was your example wot put it into his 'ead fust, I b'leeve," ses Sam, looking at Peter for 'im to notice 'ow clever he was.

"And then, Sam and Ginger Dick being teetotallers too," ses Peter, "we all, natural-like, keep together."

Mr. Goodman said they was wise men, and, arter a little more talk, he said 'ow would it be if they went out and saw a little bit of the great wicked city? They all said they would, and Ginger got quite excited about it until he found that it meant London.

They got on a bus at Aldgate, and fust of all they went to the British Museum, and when Mr. Goodman was tired o' that—and long arter the others was—they went into a place and 'ad a nice strong cup of tea and a piece o' cake each. When they come out o' there they all walked about looking at the shops until they was tired out, and arter wot Mr. Goodman said was a very improving evening they all went 'ome.

Sam and Ginger went 'ome just for the look 'o the thing, and arter waiting a few minutes in their room they crept downstairs agin to spend wot was left of the evening. They went down as quiet as mice, but, for all that, just as they was passing Mr. Goodman's room the door opened, and Peter, in a polite voice, asked 'em to step inside.

"We was just thinking you'd be dull up there all alone," he ses.

Sam lost 'is presence o' mind, and afore he knew wot 'e was doing 'im and Ginger 'ad walked in and sat down. They sat there for over an hour and a 'arf talking, and then Sam, with a look at Ginger, said they must be going, because he 'ad got to call for a pair o' boots he 'ad left to be mended.

"Why, Sam, wot are you thinking of?" ses Peter, who didn't want anybody to 'ave wot he couldn't. "Why, the shop's shut."

"I don't think so," ses Sam, glaring at 'im. "Anyway, we can go and see."

Peter said he'd go with 'im, and just as they got to the door Mr. Goodman said he'd go too. O' course, the shops was shut, and arter Mr. Goodman 'ad stood on Tower Hill admiring the Tower by moonlight till Sam felt ready to drop, they all walked back. Three times Sam's boot-lace come undone, but as the ethers all stopped too to see 'im do it up it didn't do 'im much good. Wot with temper and dryness 'e could 'ardly bid Peter "Good-night."

Sam and Ginger 'ad something the next morning, but morning ain't the time for it; and arter they had 'ad dinner Mr. Goodman asked 'em to go to the Zoological Gardens with 'im. He paid for them all, and he 'ad a lot to say about kindness to animals and 'ow you could do anything with 'em a'most by kindness. He walked about the place talking like a book, and when a fat monkey, wot was pretending to be asleep, got a bit o' Sam's whisker, he said it was on'y instink, and the animal had no wish to do 'im 'arm.

"Very likely thought it was doing you a kindness, Sam," ses Ginger.

Mr. Goodman said it was very likely, afore Sam could speak, and arter walking about and looking at the other things they come out and 'ad a nice, strong, 'ot cup o' tea, same as they 'ad the day before, and then walked about, not knowing what to do with themselves.

Sam got tired of it fust, and catching Ginger's eye said he thought it was time to get 'ome in case too much enjoyment wasn't good for 'em. His idea was to get off with Ginger and make a night of it, and when 'e found Peter and his uncle was coming too, he began to think that things was looking serious.

"I don't want to spile your evening," he says, very perlite. "I must get 'ome to mend a pair o' trowsis o' mine, but there's no need for you to come."

"I'll come and watch you," ses Peter's uncle.

"And then I'm going off to bed early," ses Sam. "Me, too," ses Ginger, and Peter said he could hardly keep 'is eyes open.

They got on a bus, and as Sam was about to foller Ginger and Peter on top, Mr. Goodman took hold of 'im by the arm and said they'd go inside. He paid two penny fares, and while Sam was wondering 'ow to tell 'im that it would be threepence each, the bus stopped to take up a passenger and he got up and moved to the door.

"They've gone up there," he ses, pointing.

Afore Sam could stop 'im he got off, and Sam, full o' surprise, got off too, and follered 'im' on to the pavement.

"Who's gone up there?" he ses, as the bus went on agin.

"Peter and Mr. Ginger Dick," ses Mr. Good-man. "But don't you trouble. You go 'ome and mend your trowsis."

"But they're on the bus," ses Sam, staring. "Dick and Peter, I mean."

Mr. Goodman shook his 'ead.

"They got off. Didn't you see 'em?" he ses. "No," ses Sam, "I'll swear they didn't."

"Well, it's my mistake, I s'pose," ses Peter's uncle. "But you get off home; I'm not tired yet, and I'll walk."

Sam said 'e wasn't very tired, and he walked along wondering whether Mr. Goodman was quite right in his 'ead. For one thing, 'e seemed upset about something or other, and kept taking little peeps at 'im in a way he couldn't understand at all.

"It was nice tea we 'ad this arternoon," ses Mr. Goodman at last.

"De-licious," ses Sam.

"Trust a teetotaller for knowing good tea," ses Mr. Goodman. "I expect Peter enjoyed it. I s'pose 'e is a very strict teetotaller?"

"Strict ain't the word for it," ses Sam, trying to do 'is duty by Peter. "We all are."

"That's right," ses Mr. Goodman, and he pushed his 'at back and looked at Sam very serious. They walked on a bit further, and then Peter's uncle stopped sudden just as they was passing a large public-'ouse and looked at Sam.

"I don't want Peter to know, 'cos it might alarm 'im," he ses, "but I've come over a bit faint. I'll go in 'ere for 'arf a minnit and sit down. You'd better wait outside."

"I'll come in with you, in case you want help," ses Sam. "I don't mind wot people think."

Mr. Goodman tried to persuade 'im not to, but it was all no good, and at last 'e walked in and sat down on a tall stool that stood agin the bar, and put his hand to his 'ead.

"I s'pose we shall 'ave to 'ave something," he ses in a whisper to Sam; "we can't expect to come in and sit down for nothing. What'll you take?"

Sam looked at 'im, but he might just as well ha' looked at a brass door-knob.

"I—I—I'll 'ave a small ginger-beer," he ses at last, "a very small one."

"One small ginger," ses Mr. Goodman to the bar-maid, "and one special Scotch."

Sam could 'ardly believe his ears, and he stood there 'oldin' his glass o' ginger-beer and watching Peter's teetotal uncle drink whiskey, and thought 'e must be dreaming.

"I dessay it seems very shocking to you," ses Mr. Goodman, putting down 'is glass and dryin' 'is lips on each other, "but I find it useful for these attacks."

"I—I s'pose the flavor's very nasty?" ses Sam, taking a sip at 'is ginger-beer.

"Not exactly wot you could call nasty," ses Mr. Goodman, "though I dessay it would seem so to you. I don't suppose you could swallow it."

"I don't s'pose I could," ses Sam, "but I've a good mind to 'ave a try. If it's good for one teetotaller I don't see why it should hurt another."

Mr. Goodman looked at 'im very hard, and then he ordered a whiskey and stood watching while Sam, arter pretending for a minnit to look at it as though 'e didn't know wot to do with it, took a sip and let it roll round 'is mouth.

"Well?" ses Mr. Goodman, looking at 'im anxious-like.

"It ain't so 'orrid as I 'ad fancied," ses Sam, lap-ping up the rest very gentle.

"'Ave you 'ad enough to do you all the good it ought to?"

Mr. Goodman said that it was no good 'arf doing a thing, and p'r'aps he 'ad better 'ave one more; and arter Sam 'ad paid for the next two they went out arm-in-arm.

"'Ow cheerful everybody looks!" ses Mr. Good-man, smiling.

"They're going to amuse theirselves, I expect," ses Sam— "music-'alls and such-like."

Mr. Goodman shook his 'ead at 'em.

"Music-'alls ain't so bad as some people try to make out," ses Sam.

"Look 'ere; I took some drink to see what the flavor was like; suppose you go to a music-'all to see wot that's like?"

"It seems on'y fair," ses Peter's uncle, considering.

"It is fair," ses Sam, and twenty minutes arterwards they was sitting in a music-'all drinking each other's 'ealths and listening to the songs— Mr. Goodman with a big cigar in 'is mouth and his 'at cocked over one eye, and Sam beating time to the music with 'is pipe.

"'Ow do you like it?" he ses.

Mr. Goodman didn't answer 'im because 'e was joining in the chorus with one side of 'is mouth and keeping 'is cigar alight with the other. He just nodded at 'im; but 'e looked so 'appy that Sam felt it was a pleasure to sit there and look at 'im.

"I wonder wot Peter and Ginger is doin'?" he ses, when the song was finished.

"I don't know," ses Mr. Goodman, "and, wot's more, I don't care. If I'd 'ad any idea that Peter was like wot he is I should never 'ave wrote to 'im. I can't think 'ow you can stand 'im."

"He ain't so bad," ses Sam, wondering whether he ought to tell 'im 'arf of wot Peter really was like.

"Bad!" ses Mr. Goodman. "I come up to London for a 'oliday—a change, mind you—and I thought Peter and me was going to 'ave a good time. Instead o' that, he goes about with a face as long as a fiddle. He don't drink, 'e don't go to places of amusement—innercent places of amusement —and 'is idea of enjoying life is to go walking about the streets and drinking cups o' tea."

"We must try and alter 'im," ses Sam, arter doing a bit o' thinking.

"Certainly not," ses Mr. Goodman, laying his 'and on Sam's knee. "Far be it from me to interfere with a feller-creature's ideas o' wot's right. Besides, he might get writing to 'is sister agin, and she might tell my wife."

"But Peter said she was dead," ses Sam, very puzzled.

"I married agin," ses Peter's uncle, in a whisper, 'cos people was telling 'im to keep quiet, "a tartar— a perfect tartar. She's in a 'orsepittle at present, else I shouldn't be 'ere. And I shouldn't ha' been able to come if I 'adn't found five pounds wot she'd hid in a match-box up the chimbley."

"But wot'll you do when she finds it out?" ses Sam, opening 'is eyes.

"I'm going to 'ave the house cleaned and the chimbleys swept to welcome her 'ome," ses Mr. Goodman, taking a sip o' whiskey. "It'll be a little surprise for her."

They stayed till it was over, and on the bus he gave Sam some strong peppermint lozenges wot 'e always carried about with 'im, and took some 'imself. He said 'e found 'em helpful.

"What are we going to tell Peter and Ginger?" ses Sam, as they got near the 'ouse.

"Tell 'em?" ses Mr. Goodman. "Tell 'em the truth. How we follered 'em when they got off the bus, and 'ave been looking for 'em ever since. I'm not going to 'ave my 'oliday spoilt by a teetotal nevvy, I can tell you."

He started on Peter, wot was sitting on his bed with Ginger waiting for them, the moment he got inside, and all Ginger and Peter could say didn't make any difference.

"Mr. Small see you as plain as what I did," he ses.

"Plainer," ses Sam.

"But I tell you we come straight 'ome," ses Ginger, "and we've been waiting for you 'ere ever since."

Mr. Goodman shook his 'ead at 'im. "Say no more about it," he ses, in a kind voice. "I dessay it's rather tiresome for young men to go about with two old ones, and in future, if you and Peter keep together, me and my friend Mr. Small will do the same."

Sam shook 'ands with 'im, and though Peter tried his 'ardest to make 'im alter his mind it was no good. His uncle patted 'im on the shoulder, and said they'd try it for a few days, at any rate, and Ginger, wot thought it was a very good idea, backed 'im up. Everybody seemed pleased with the idea except Peter Russet, but arter Sam 'ad told 'im in private wot a high opinion 'is uncle 'ad got of 'im, and 'ow well off he was, 'e gave way.

They all enjoyed the next evening, and Sam and Mr. Goodman got on together like twin brothers. They went to a place of amusement every night, and the on'y unpleasantness that happened was when Peter's uncle knocked a chemist's shop up at a quarter-past twelve one night to buy a penn'orth o' peppermint lozenges.

They 'ad four of the 'appiest evenings together that Sam 'ad ever known; and Mr. Goodman would 'ave been just as 'appy too if it hadn't ha' been for the thoughts o' that five pounds. The more 'e thought of it the more unlikely it seemed that 'is wife would blame it on to the sweep, and one night he took the match-box out of 'is pocket and shook his 'ead over it till Sam felt quite sorry for 'im.

"Don't take up your troubles afore they come," he ses. "Orsepittles are dangerous places."

Mr. Goodman cheered up a bit at that, but he got miserable agin the next night because 'is money was getting low and he wanted another week in London.

"I've got seven shillings and fourpence and two stamps left," he ses. "Where it's all gone to I can't think."

"Don't you worry about that," ses Sam. "I've got a pound or two left yet."

"No, I ain't going to be a burden on you," ses Mr. Goodman, "but another week I must 'ave, so I must get the money somehow. Peter can't spend much, the way he goes on."

Sam gave a little cough.

"I'll get a pound or two out of 'im," ses Mr. Goodman.

Sam coughed agin. "Won't he think it rather funny?" he ses, arter a bit.

"Not if it's managed properly," ses Mr. Good-man, thinking 'ard. "I'll tell you 'ow we'll do it. To-morrow morning, while we are eating of our breakfast, you ask me to lend you a pound or two."

Sam, what 'ad just taken up 'is glass for a drink, put it down agin and stared at 'im.

"But I don't want no money," he ses; "and, besides, you 'aven't got any."

"You do as I tell you," ses Mr. Goodman, "and when you've got it, you hand it over to me, see? Ask me to lend you five pounds."

Sam thought as 'ow the whiskey 'ad got to Mr. Goodman's 'ead at last. 'Owever, to pacify 'im he promised to do wot 'e was told, and next morning, when they was all at breakfast, he looks over and catches Mr. Goodman's eye.

"I wonder if I might be so bold as to ask a favor of you?" he ses.

"Certainly," ses Peter's uncle, "and glad I shall be to oblige you. There is no man I've got a greater respect for."

"Thankee," ses Sam. "The fact is, I've run a bit short owing to paying a man some money I owed 'im. If you could lend me five pounds, I couldn't thank you enough."

Mr. Goodman put down 'is knife and fork and wrinkled up 'is forehead.

"I'm very sorry," he ses, feeling in 'is pockets; "do you want it to-day?"

"Yes; I should like it," ses Sam.

"It's most annoying," ses Mr. Goodman, "but I was so afraid o' pickpockets that I didn't bring much away with me. If you could wait till the day arter to-morrow, when my money is sent to me, you can 'ave ten if you like."

"You're very kind," ses Sam, "but that 'ud be too late for me. I must try and get it somewhere else." Peter and Ginger went on eating their breakfast, but every time Peter looked up he caught 'is uncle looking at 'im in such a surprised and disappointed sort o' way that 'e didn't like the look of it at all.

"I could just do it for a couple o' days, Sam," he ses at last, "but it'll leave me very short."

"That's right," ses his uncle, smiling. "My nevvy, Peter Russet, will lend it to you, Mr. Small, of 'is own free will. He 'as offered afore he was asked, and that's the proper way to do it, in my opinion."

He reached acrost the table and shook 'ands with Peter, and said that generosity ran in their family, and something seemed to tell 'im as Peter wouldn't lose by it. Everybody seemed pleased with each other, and arter Ginger Dick and Peter 'ad gone out Mr. Goodman took the five pounds off of old Sam and stowed 'em away very careful in the match-box.

"It's nice to 'ave money agin," he ses. "There's enough for a week's enjoyment here."

"Yes," ses Sam, slow-like; "but wot I want to know is, wot about the day arter to-morrow, when Peter expects 'is money?"

Mr. Goodman patted 'im on the shoulder. "Don't you worry about Peter's troubles," he ses. "I know exactly wot to do; it's all planned out. Now I'm going to 'ave a lay down for an hour—I didn't get much sleep last night—and if you'll call me at twelve o'clock we'll go somewhere. Knock loud."

He patted 'im on the shoulder agin, and Sam, arter fidgeting about a bit, went out. The last time he ever see Peter's uncle he was laying on the bed with 'is eyes shut, smiling in his sleep. And Peter Russet didn't see Sam for eighteen months.

There was a sudden uproar on deck, and angry shouts, accompanied by an incessant barking; the master of the brig Arethusa stopped with his knife midway to his mouth, and exchanging glances with the mate, put it down and rose to his feet.

"They're chevying that poor animal again," he said hotly. "It's scandalous."

"Rupert can take care of himself," said the mate calmly, continuing his meal. "I expect, if the truth's known, it's him 's been doin' the chevying."

"You're as bad as the rest of 'em," said the skipper angrily, as a large brown retriever came bounding into the cabin. "Poor old Rupe! what have they been doin' to you?"

The dog, with a satisfied air, sat down panting by his chair, listening quietly to the subdued hubbub which sounded from the companion.

"Well, what is it?" roared the skipper, patting his favourite's head.

"It's that blasted dawg, sir," cried an angry voice from above. "Go down and show 'im your leg, Joe."

"An' 'ave another lump took out of it, I s'pose," said another voice sourly. "Not me."

"I don't want to look at no legs while I'm at dinner," cried the skipper. "O' course the dog 'll bite you if you've been teasing him."

"There's nobody been teasing 'im," said the angry voice again. "That's the second one 'e's bit, and now Joe's goin' to have 'im killed—ain't you, Joe?"

Joe's reply was not audible, although the infuriated skipper was straining his ears to catch it.

"Who's going to have the dog killed?" he demanded, going up on deck, while Rupert, who evidently thought he had an interest in the proceedings, followed unobtrusively behind.

"I am, sir," said Joe Bates, who was sitting on the hatch while the cook bathed an ugly wound in his leg. "A dog's only allowed one bite, and he's 'ad two this week."

"He bit me on Monday," said the seaman who had spoken before. "Now he's done for hisself."

"Hold your tongue!" said the skipper angrily. "You think you know a lot about the law, Sam Clark; let me tell you a dog's entitled to have as many bites as ever he likes, so as he don't bite the same person twice."

"That ain't the way I've 'eard it put afore," said Clark, somewhat taken back.

"He's the cutest dog breathing," said the skipper fondly, "and he knows all about it. He won't bite either of you again."

"And wot about them as 'asn't been bit yet, sir?" inquired the cook.

"Don't halloo before you're hurt," advised the skipper. "If you don't tease him he won't bite you."

He went down to his dinner, followed by the sagacious Rupert, leaving the hands to go forward again, and to mutinously discuss a situation which was fast becoming unbearable.

"It can't go on no longer, Joe," said Clark firmly; "this settles it."

"Where is the stuff?" inquired the cook in a whisper.

"In my chest," said Clark softly. "I bought it the night he bit me."

"It's a risky thing to do," said Bates.

"'Ow risky?" asked Sam scornfully. "The dog eats the stuff and dies. Who's going to say what he died of? As for suspicions, let the old man suspect as much as he likes. It ain't proof."

The stronger mind had its way, as usual, and the next day the skipper, coming quietly on deck, was just in time to see Joe Bates throw down a fine fat bloater in front of the now amiable Rupert. He covered the distance between himself and the dog in three bounds, and seizing it by the neck, tore the fish from its eager jaws and held it aloft.

"I just caught 'im in the act!" he cried, as the mate came on deck. "What did you give that to my dog for?" he inquired of the conscience-stricken Bates.

"I wanted to make friends with him," stammered the other.

"It's poisoned, you rascal, and you know it," said the skipper vehemently.

"Wish I may die, sir," began Joe.

"That'll do," said the skipper harshly. "You've tried to poison my dog."

"I ain't," said Joe firmly.

"You ain't been trying to kill 'im with a poisoned bloater?" demanded the skipper.

"Certainly not, sir," said Joe. "I wouldn't do such a thing. I couldn't if I tried."

"Very good then," said the skipper; "if it's all right you eat it, and I'll beg your pardon."

"I ain't goin' to eat after a dog," said Joe, shuffling.

"The dog's as clean as you are," said the skipper. "I'd sooner eat after him than you."

"Well, you eat it then, sir," said Bates desperately. "If it's poisoned you'll die, and I'll be 'ung for it. I can't say no fairer than that, can I?"

There was a slight murmur from the men, who stood by watching the skipper with an air of unholy expectancy.

"Well, the boy shall eat it then," said the skipper. "Eat that bloater, boy, and I'll give you sixpence."

The boy came forward slowly, and looking from the men to the skipper, and from the skipper back to the men, began to whimper.

"If you think it's poisoned," interrupted the mate, "you oughtn't to make the boy eat it. I don't like boys, but you must draw the line somewhere."

"It's poisoned," said the skipper, shaking it at Bates, "and they know it. Well, I'll keep it till we get to port, and then I'll have it analysed. And it'll be a sorry day for you, Bates, when I hear it's poisoned. A month's hard labour is what you'll get."

He turned away and went below with as much dignity as could be expected of a man carrying a mangled herring, and placing it on a clean plate, solemnly locked it up in his state-room.

For two days the crew heard no more about it, though the skipper's eyes gleamed dangerously each time that they fell upon the shrinking Bates. The weather was almost tropical, with not an air stirring, and the Arethusa, bearing its dread secret still locked in its state-room, rose and fell upon a sea of glassy smoothness without making any progress worth recording.

"I wish you'd keep that thing in your berth, George," said the skipper, as they sat at tea the second evening; "it puts me in a passion every time I look at it."

"I couldn't think of it, cap'n," replied the mate firmly; "it makes me angry enough as it is. Every time I think of 'em trying to poison that poor dumb creature I sort o' choke. I try to forget it."

The skipper, eyeing him furtively, helped himself to another cup of tea.

"You haven't got a tin box with a lid to it, I s'pose?" he remarked somewhat shamefacedly.

The mate shook his head. "I looked for one this morning," he said. "There ain't so much as a bottle aboard we could shove it into, and it wants shoving into something—bad, it does."

"I don't like to be beat," said the skipper, shaking his head. "All them grinning monkeys for'ard 'ud think it a rare good joke. I'd throw it overboard if it wasn't for that. We can't keep it this weather."

"Well, look 'ere; 'ere's a way out of it," said the mate. "Call Joe down, and make him keep it in the foc'sle and take care of it. That'll punish 'em all too."

"Why, you idiot, he'd lose it!" rapped out the other impatiently.

"O' course he would," said the mate; "but that's the most digernified way out of it for you. You can call 'im all sorts o' things, and abuse 'im for the rest of his life. They'll prove themselves guilty by chucking it away, won't they?"

It really seemed the only thing to be done. The skipper finished his tea in silence, and then going on deck called the crew aft and apprised them of his intentions, threatening them with all sorts of pains and penalties if the treasure about to be confided to their keeping should be lost The cook was sent below for it, and, at the skipper's bidding, handed it to the grinning Joe.

"And mind," said the skipper as he turned away, "I leave it in your keepin', and if it's missing I shall understand that you've made away with it, and I shall take it as a sign of guilt, and act according."

The end came sooner even than he expected. They were at breakfast next morning when Joe, looking somewhat pale, came down to the cabin, followed by Clark, bearing before him an empty plate.

"Well?" said the skipper fiercely.

"It's about the 'erring, sir," said Joe, twisting his cap between his hands.

"Well?" roared the skipper again.

"It's gone, sir," said Joe, in bereaved accents.

"You mean you've thrown it away, you infernal rascal!" bellowed the skipper.

"No, sir," said Joe.

"Ah! I s'pose it walked up on deck and jumped overboard," said the mate.

"No, sir," said Joe softly. "The dog ate it, sir."

The skipper swung round in his seat and regarded him open-mouthed.

"The—dog—ate—it?" he repeated.

"Yes, sir; Clark saw 'im do it—didn't you, Clark?"

"I did," said Clark promptly. He had made his position doubly sure by throwing it overboard himself.

"It comes to the same thing, sir," said Joe sanctimoniously; "my innercence is proved just the same. You'll find the dog won't take no 'urt through it, sir. You watch 'im."

The skipper breathed hard, but made no reply.

"If you don't believe me, sir, p'raps you'd like to see the plate where 'e licked it?" said Joe. "Give me the plate, Sam."

He turned to take it, but in place of handing it to him that useful witness dropped it and made hurriedly for the companion-ladder, and by strenuous efforts reached the deck before Joe, although that veracious gentleman, assisted from below by strong and willing arms, made a good second.

PRIVATE CLOTHES

At half-past nine the crew of the Merman were buried in slumber, at nine thirty-two three of the members were awake with heads protruding out of their bunks, trying to peer through the gloom, while the fourth dreamt that a tea-tray was falling down a never-ending staircase. On the floor of the forecastle something was cursing prettily and rubbing itself.

"Did you 'ear anything, Ted?" inquired a voice in an interval of silence.

"Who is it?" demanded Ted, ignoring the question. "Wot d'yer want?"

"I'll let you know who I am," said a thick and angry voice. "I've broke my blarsted back."

"Light the lamp, Bill," said Ted.

Bill struck a tandsticker match, and carefully nursing the tiny sulphurous flame with his hand, saw dimly some high-coloured object on the floor.

He got out of his bunk and lit the lamp, and an angry and very drunken member of Her Majesty's foot forces became visible.

"Wot are you doin' 'ere?" inquired Ted, sharply, "this ain't the guard-room."

"Who knocked me over?" demanded the soldier sternly; "take your co—coat off lik' a man."

He rose to his feet and swayed unsteadily to and fro.

"If you keep your li'l' 'eads still," he said gravely, to Bill, "I'll punch 'em."

By a stroke of good fortune he selected the real head, and gave it a blow which sent it crashing against the woodwork. For a moment the seaman stood gathering his scattered senses, then with an oath he sprang forward, and in the lightest of fighting trim waited until his adversary, who was by this time on the floor again, should have regained his feet.

"He's drunk, Bill," said another voice, "don't 'urt 'im. He's a chap wot said 'e was coming aboard to see me—I met 'im in the Green Man this evening. You was coming to see me, mate, wasn't you?"

The soldier looked up stupidly, and gripping hold of the injured Bill by the shirt, staggered to his feet again, and advancing towards the last speaker let fly suddenly in his face.

"Sort man I am," he said, autobiographically. "Feel my arm."

The indignant Bill took him by both, and throwing himself upon him suddenly fell with him to the floor. The intruder's head met the boards with a loud crash, and then there was silence.

"You ain't killed 'im, Bill?" said an old seaman, stooping over him anxiously.

"Course not," was the reply; "give us some water."

He threw some in the soldier's face, and then poured some down his neck, but with no result. Then he stood upright, and exchanged glances of consternation with his friends.

"I don't like the way he's breathing," he said, in a trembling voice.

"You always was pertikler, Bill," said the cook, who had thankfully got to the bottom of his staircase. "If I was you—"

He was not allowed to proceed any further; footsteps and a voice were heard above, and as old Thomas hastily extinguished the lamp, the mate's head was thrust down the scuttle, and the mate's voice sounded a profane reveillé.

"Wot are we goin' to do with it?" inquired Ted, as the mate walked away.

"I'm, Ted," said Bill, nervously. "He's alive all right."

"If we put 'im ashore an' 'e's dead," said old Thomas, "there'll be trouble for somebody. Better let 'im be, and if 'e's dead, why we don't none of us know nothing about it."

The men ran up on deck, and Bill, being the last to leave, put a boot under the soldier's head before he left. Ten minutes later they were under way, and standing about the deck, discussed the situation in thrilling whispers as opportunity offered.

At breakfast, by which time they were in a dirty tumbling sea, with the Nore lightship, a brown, forlorn-looking object on their beam, the soldier, who had been breathing stertorously, raised his heavy head from the boot, and with glassy eyes and tightly compressed lips gazed wonderingly about him.

"Wot cheer, mate?" said the delighted Bill. "'Ow goes it?"

"Where am I?" inquired Private Harry Bliss, in a weak voice.

"Brig Merman," said Bill; "bound for Byster-mouth."

"Well, I'm damned," said Private Bliss; "it's a blooming miracle. Open the winder, it's a bit stuffy down here. Who—who brought me here?"

"You come to see me last night," said Bob, "an' fell down, I s'pose; then you punched Bill 'ere in the eye and me in the jor."

Mr. Bliss, still feeling very sick and faint, turned to Bill, and after critically glancing at the eye turned on him for inspection, transferred his regards to the other man's jaw.

"I'm a devil when I'm boozed," he said, in a satisfied voice. "Well, I must get ashore; I shall get cells for this, I expect."

He staggered to the ladder, and with unsteady haste gained the deck and made for the side. The heaving waters made him giddy to look at, and he gazed for preference at a thin line of coast stretching away in the distance.

The startled mate, who was steering, gave him a hail, but he made no reply. A little fishing-boat was jumping about in a way to make a sea-sick man crazy, and he closed his eyes with a groan.

Then the skipper, aroused by the mate's hail, came up from below, and walking up to him put a heavy hand on his shoulder.

"What are you doing aboard this ship?" he demanded, austerely.

"Go away," said Private Bliss, faintly; "take your paw off my tunic; you'll spoil it."

He clung miserably to the side, leaving the incensed skipper to demand explanations from the crew. The crew knew nothing about him, and said that he must have stowed himself away in an empty bunk; the skipper pointed out coarsely that there were no empty bunks, whereupon Bill said that he had not occupied his the previous evening, but had fallen asleep sitting on the locker, and had injured his eye against the corner of a bunk in consequence. In proof whereof he produced the eye.

"Look here, old man," said Private Bliss, who suddenly felt better. He turned and patted the skipper on the back. "You just turn to the left a bit and put me ashore, will you?"

"I'll put you ashore at Bystermouth," said the skipper, with a grin. "You're a deserter, that's what you are, and I'll take care you're took care of."

"You put me ashore!" roared Private Bliss, with a very fine imitation of the sergeant-major's parade voice.

"Get out and walk," said the skipper contemptuously, over his shoulder, as he walked off.

"Here," said Mr. Bliss, unbuckling his belt, "hold my tunic one of you. I'll learn 'im."

Before the paralysed crew could prevent him he had flung his coat into Bill's arms and followed the master of the Merman aft. As a light-weight he was rather fancied at the gymnasium, and in the all too brief exhibition which followed he displayed fine form and a knowledge of anatomy which even the skipper's tailor was powerless to frustrate.

The frenzy of the skipper as Ted assisted him to his feet and he saw his antagonist struggling in the arms of the crew was terrible to behold. Strong men shivered at his words, but Mr. Bliss, addressing him as "Whiskers," told him to call his crew off and to come on, and shaping as well as two pairs of brawny arms round his middle would permit, endeavoured in vain to reach him.

"This," said the skipper, bitterly, as he turned to the mate, "is what you an' me have to pay to keep up. I wouldn't let you go now, my lad, not for a fi' pun' note. Deserter, that's what you are!"

He turned and went below, and Private Bliss, after an insulting address to the mate, was hauled forward, struggling fiercely, and seated on the deck to recover. The excitement passed, he lost his colour again, and struggling into his tunic, went and brooded over the side.

By dinner-time his faintness had passed, and he sniffed with relish at the smell from the galley. The cook emerged bearing dinner to the cabin, then he returned and took a fine smoking piece of boiled beef flanked with carrots down to the forecastle. Private Bliss eyed him wistfully and his mouth watered.

For a time pride struggled with hunger, then pride won a partial victory and he descended carelessly to the forecastle.

"Can any o' you chaps lend me a pipe o' baccy?" he asked, cheerfully.

Bill rummaged in his pocket and found a little tobacco in a twist of paper.

"Bad thing to smoke on a empty stomach," he said, with his mouth full.

"'Tain't my fault it's empty," said Private Bliss, pathetically.

"Tain't mine," said Bill.

"I've 'eard," said the cook, who was a tenderhearted man, "as 'ow it's a good thing to go for a day or so without food sometimes."

"Who said so?" inquired Private Bliss, hotly.

"Diff'rent people," replied the cook.

"You can tell 'em from me they're blamed fools," said Mr. Bliss.

There was an uncomfortable silence; Mr. Bliss lit his pipe, but it did not seem to draw well.

"Did you like that pot o' six-half I stood you last night?" he inquired somewhat pointedly of Bob.

Bob hesitated and looked at his plate.

"No, it was a bit flat," he said at length.

"Well, I won't stop you chaps at your grub," said Private Bliss, bitterly, as he turned to depart.

"You're not stopping us," said Ted, cheerfully. "I'd offer you a bit, only—"

"Only what?" demanded the other.

"Skipper's orders," said Ted. "He ses we're not to. He ses if we do it's helping a deserter, and we'll all get six months."

"But you're helping me by having me on board," said Private Bliss; "besides, I don't want to desert."

"We couldn't 'elp you coming aboard," said Bill, "that's wot the old man said, but 'e ses we can 'elp giving of him vittles, he ses."

"Well, have I got to starve?" demanded the horror-stricken Mr. Bliss.

"Look 'ere," said Bill, frankly, "go and speak to the old man. It's no good talking to us. Go and have it out with him."

Private Bliss thanked him and went on deck. Old Thomas was at the wheel, and a pleasant clatter of knives and forks came up through the open skylight of the cabin. Ignoring the old man, who waved him away, he raised the open skylight still higher, and thrust his head in.

"Go away," bawled the skipper, pausing with his knife in his fist as he caught sight of him.

"I want to know where I'm to have my dinner," bawled back the thoroughly roused Mr. Bliss.

"Your dinner!" said the skipper, with an air of surprise; "why, I didn't know you 'ad any."

Private Bliss took his head away, and holding it very erect, took in his belt a little and walked slowly up and down the deck. Then he went to the water-cask and took a long drink, and an hour later a generous message was received from the skipper that he might have as many biscuits as he liked.

On this plain fare Private Bliss lived the whole of that day and the next, snatching a few hours' troubled sleep on the locker at nights. His peace of mind was by no means increased by the information of Ted that Bystermouth was a garrison town, and feeling that in spite of any explanation he would be treated as a deserter, he resolved to desert in good earnest at the first opportunity that offered.

By the third day nobody took any notice of him, and his presence on board was almost forgotten, until Bob, going down to the forecastle, created a stir by asking somewhat excitedly what had become of him.

"He's on deck, I s'pose," said the cook, who was having a pipe.

"He's not," said Bob, solemnly.

"He's not gone overboard, I s'pose?" said Bill, starting up.

Touched by this morbid suggestion they went up on deck and looked round; Private Bliss was nowhere to be seen, and Ted, who was steering, Had heard no splash. He seemed to have disappeared by magic, and the cook, after a hurried search, ventured aft, and, descending to the cabin, mentioned his fears to the skipper.

"Nonsense!" said that gentleman, sharply, "I'll lay I'll find him."

He came on deck and looked round, followed at a respectful distance by the crew, but there was no sign of Mr. Bliss.

Then an idea, a horrid idea, occurred to the cook. The colour left his cheeks and he gazed helplessly at the skipper.

"What is it?" bawled the latter.

The cook, incapable of speech, raised a trembling hand and pointed to the galley. The skipper started, and, rushing to the door, drew it hastily back.

Mr. Bliss had apparently finished, though he still toyed languidly with his knife and fork as though loath to put them down. A half-emptied saucepan of potatoes stood on the floor by his side, and a bone, with a small fragment of meat adhering, was between his legs on a saucepan lid which served as a dish.

"Rather underdone, cook," he said, severely, as he met that worthy's horror-stricken gaze.

"Is that the cabin's or the men's he's eaten?" vociferated the skipper.

"Cabin's," replied Mr. Bliss, before the cook could speak; "it looked the best. Now, has anybody got a nice see-gar?"

He drew back the door the other side of the galley as he spoke, and went out that way. A move was made towards him, but he backed, and picking up a handspike swung it round his head.

"Let him be," said the skipper in a choking voice, "let him be. He'll have to answer for stealing my dinner when I get 'im ashore. Cook, take the men's dinner down into the cabin. I'll talk to you by and by."

He walked aft and disappeared below, while Private Bliss, still fondling the handspike, listened unmoved to a lengthy vituperation which Bill called a plain and honest opinion of his behaviour.

"It's the last dinner you'll 'ave for some time," he concluded, spitefully; "it'll be skilly for you when you get ashore."

Mr. Bliss smiled, and, fidgeting with his tongue, asked him for the loan of his toothpick.

"You won't be using it yourself," he urged. "Now you go below all of you and start on the biscuits, there's good men. It's no use standing there saying a lot o' bad words what I left off when I was four years old."

He filled his pipe with some tobacco he had thoughtfully borrowed from the cook before dinner, and dropping into a negligent attitude on the deck, smoked placidly with his eyes half-closed. The brig was fairly steady and the air hot and slumberous, and with an easy assurance that nobody would hit him while in that position, he allowed his head to fall on his chest and dropped off into a light sleep.

It became evident to him the following afternoon that they were nearing Bystermouth. The skipper contented himself with eyeing him with an air of malicious satisfaction, but the crew gratified themselves by painting the horrors of his position in strong colors. Private Bliss affected indifference, but listened eagerly to all they had to say, with the air of a general considering his enemy's plans.

It was a source of disappointment to the crew that they did not arrive until after nightfall, and the tide was already too low for them to enter the harbour. They anchored outside, and Private Bliss, despite his position, felt glad as he smelt the land again, and saw the twinkling lights and houses ashore. He could even hear the clatter of a belated vehicle driving along the seafront. Lights on the summits of the heights in the background, indicated, so Bill said, the position of the fort.

To the joy of the men he partly broke down in the forecastle that night; and, in tropical language, severally blamed his parents, the School Board, and the Army for not having taught him to swim. The last thing that Bill heard, ere sleep closed his lids, was a pious resolution on the part of Mr. Bliss to the effect that all his children should be taught the art of natation as soon as they were born.

Bill woke up just before six; and, hearing a complaining voice, thought at first that his military friend was still speaking. The voice got more and more querulous with occasional excursions into the profane, and the seaman, rubbing his eyes, turned his head, and saw old Thomas groping about the forecastle.

"Wot's the matter with you, old 'un?" he demanded.

"I can't find my trousis," grumbled the old man.

"Did you 'ave 'em on larst night?" inquired Bill, who was still half asleep.

"Course I did, you fool," said the other snappishly.

"Be civil," said Bill, calmly, "be civil. Are you sure you haven't got 'em on now?"

The old man greeted this helpful suggestion with such a volley of abuse that Bill lost his temper.

"P'r'aps somebody's got 'em on their bed, thinking they was a patchwork quilt," he said, coldly; "it's a mistake anybody might make. Have you got the jacket?"

"I ain't got nothing," replied the bewildered old man, "'cept wot I stand up in."

"That ain't much," said Bill frankly. "Where's that blooming sojer?" he demanded suddenly.

"I don't know where 'e is, and I don't care," replied the old man. "On deck, I s'pose."

"P'r'aps 'e's got 'em on," said the unforgiving Bill; "'e didn't seem a very pertikler sort of chap."

The old man started, and hurriedly ascended to the deck. He was absent two or three minutes, and, when he returned, consternation was writ large upon his face.

"He's gone," he spluttered; "there ain't a sign of 'im about, and the life-belt wot hangs on the galley 'as gone too. Wot am I to do?"

"Well, they was very old cloes," said Bill, soothingly, "an' you ain't a bad figger, not for your time o' life, Thomas."

"There's many a wooden-legged man 'ud be glad to change with you," affirmed Ted, who had been roused by the noise. "You'll soon get over the feeling o' shyness, Thomas."

The forecastle laughed encouragingly, and Thomas, who had begun to realise the position, joined in. He laughed till the tears ran down his cheeks, and his excitement began to alarm his friends.

"Don't be a fool, Thomas," said Bob, anxiously.

"I can't help it," said the old man, struggling hysterically; "it's the best joke I've heard."

"He's gone dotty," said Ted, solemnly. "I never 'eard of a man larfing like that a 'cos he'd lorst 'is cloes."

"I'm not larfing at that," said Thomas, regaining his composure by a great effort. "I'm larfing at a joke wot you don't know of yet."

A deadly chill struck at the hearts of the listeners at these words, then Bill, after a glance at the foot of his bunk, where he usually kept his clothes, sprang out and began a hopeless search. The other men followed suit, and the air rang with lamentations and profanity. Even the spare suits in the men's chests had gone; and Bill, a prey to acute despair, sat down, and in a striking passage consigned the entire British Army to perdition.

"'E's taken one suit and chucked the rest overboard, I expect, so as we sha'n't be able to go arter 'im," said Thomas. "I expect he could swim arter all, Bill."

Bill, still busy with the British Army, paid no heed.

"We must go an' tell the old man," said Ted.

"Better be careful," cautioned the cook. "'Im an' the mate 'ad a go at the whisky last night, an' you know wot 'e is next morning."

The men went up slowly on deck. The morning was fine, but the air, chill with a breeze from the land, had them at a disadvantage. Ashore, a few people were early astir.

"You go down, Thomas, you're the oldest," said Bill.

"I was thinking o' Ted going," said Thomas, "'e's the youngest."

Ted snorted derisively. "Oh, was you?" he remarked helpfully.

"Or Bob," said the old man, "don't matter which."

"Toss up for it," said the cook.

Bill, who was keeping his money in his hand as the only safe place left to him, produced a penny and spun it in the air.

"Wait a bit," said Ted, earnestly. "Wot time was you to call the old man?" he asked, turning to the cook.

"Toss up for it," repeated that worthy, hurriedly.

"Six o'clock," said Bob, speaking for him; "it's that now, cookie. Better go an' call 'im at once."

"I dassent go like this," said the trembling cook.

"Well, you'll 'ave to," said Bill. "If the old man misses the tide, you know wot you've got to expect."

"Let's follow 'im down," said Ted. "Come along, cookie, we'll see you righted."

The cook thanked him, and, followed by the others, led the way down to interview the skipper. The clock ticked on the mantlepiece, and heavy snoring proceeded both from the mate's bunk and the state-room. On the door of the latter the cook knocked gently; then he turned the handle and peeped in.

The skipper, raising a heavy head, set in matted hair and disordered whiskers, glared at him fiercely.

"What d'ye want?" he roared.

"If you please, sir—" began the cook.

He opened the door as he spoke, and disclosed the lightly-clad crowd behind. The skipper's eyes grew large and his jaw dropped, while inarticulate words came from his parched and astonished throat; and the mate, who was by this time awake, sat up in his bunk and cursed them roundly for their indelicacy.

"Get out," roared the skipper, recovering his voice.

"We came to tell you," interposed Bill, "as 'ow—"

"Get out," roared the skipper again. "How dare you come to my state-room, and like this, too."

"All our clothes 'ave gone and so 'as the sojer chap," said Bill.

"Serve you damned well right for letting him go," cried the skipper, angrily. "Hurry up, George, and get alongside," he called to the mate, "we'll catch him yet. Clear out, you—you—ballet girls."

The indignant seamen withdrew slowly, and, reaching the foot of the companion, stood there in mutinous indecision. Then, as the cook placed his foot on the step, the skipper was heard calling to the mate again.

"George?" he said, in an odd voice.

"Well?" was the reply.

"I hope you're not forgetting yourself and playing larks," said the skipper, with severity.

"Larks?" repeated the mate, as the alarmed crew fled silently on deck and stood listening open-mouthed at the companion. "Of course I ain't. You don't mean to tell me—"

"All my clothes have gone, every stitch I've got," replied the skipper, desperately, as the mate sprang out. "I shall have to borrow some of yours. If I catch that infernal—"

"You're quite welcome," said the mate, bitterly, "only somebody has borrowed 'em already. That's what comes of sleeping too heavy."

The Merman sailed bashfully into harbour half an hour later, the uniforms of its crew evoking severe comment from the people on the quay. At the same time, Mr. Harry Bliss, walking along the road some ten miles distant, was trying to decide upon his future career, his present calling of "shipwrecked sailor" being somewhat too hazardous even for his bold spirit.

PRIZE MONEY

The old man stood by the window, gazing at the frozen fields beyond. The sign of the Cauliflower was stiff with snow, and the breath of a pair of waiting horses in a wagon beneath ascended in clouds of steam.

"Amusements" he said slowly, as he came back with a shiver and, resuming his seat by the tap-room fire, looked at the wayfarer who had been idly questioning him. "Claybury men don't have much time for amusements. The last one I can call to mind was Bill Chambers being nailed up in a pig-sty he was cleaning out, but there was such a fuss made over that —by Bill—that it sort o' disheartened people."

He got up again restlessly, and, walking round the table, gazed long and hard into three or four mugs.

"Sometimes a little gets left in them," he explained, meeting the stranger's inquiring glance. The latter started, and, knocking on the table with the handle of his knife, explained that he had been informed by a man outside that his companion was the bitterest teetotaller in Claybury.

"That's one o' Bob Pretty's larks," said the old man, flushing. "I see you talking to 'im, and I thought as 'ow he warn't up to no good. Biggest rascal in Claybury, he is. I've said so afore, and I'll say so agin."

He bowed to the donor and buried his old face in the mug.

"A poacher!" he said, taking breath. "A thief!" he continued, after another draught. "I wonder whether Smith spilt any of this a-carrying of it in?"

He put down the empty mug and made a careful examination of the floor, until a musical rapping on the table brought the landlord into the room again.

"My best respects," he said, gratefully, as he placed the mug on the settle by his side and slowly filled a long clay pipe. Next time you see Bob Pretty ask 'im wot happened to the prize hamper. He's done a good many things has Bob, but it'll be a long time afore Claybury men'll look over that.

It was Henery Walker's idea. Henery 'ad been away to see an uncle of 'is wife's wot had money and nobody to leave it to—leastways, so Henery thought when he wasted his money going over to see 'im—and he came back full of the idea, which he 'ad picked up from the old man.

"We each pay twopence a week till Christmas," he ses, "and we buy a hamper with a goose or a turkey in it, and bottles o' rum and whiskey and gin, as far as the money'll go, and then we all draw lots for it, and the one that wins has it."

It took a lot of explaining to some of 'em, but Smith, the landlord, helped Henery, and in less than four days twenty-three men had paid their tuppences to Henery, who 'ad been made the seckitary, and told him to hand them over to Smith in case he lost his memory.

Bob Pretty joined one arternoon on the quiet, and more than one of 'em talked of 'aving their money back, but, arter Smith 'ad explained as 'ow he would see fair play, they thought better of it.

"He'll 'ave the same chance as all of you," he ses. "No more and no less."

"I'd feel more easy in my mind, though, if'e wasn't in it," ses Bill Chambers, staring at Bob. "I never knew 'im to lose anything yet."

"You don't know everything, Bill," ses Bob, shaking his 'ead. "You don't know me; else you wouldn't talk like that. I've never been caught doing wrong yet, and I 'ope I never shall."

"It's all right, Bill," ses George Kettle. "Mr. Smith'll see fair, and I'd sooner win Bob Pretty's money than anybody's."

"I 'ope you will, mate," ses Bob; "that's what I joined for."

"Bob's money is as good as anybody else's," ses George Kettle, looking round at the others. "It don't signify to me where he got it from."

"Ah, I don't like to hear you talk like that George," ses Bob Pretty. "I've thought more than once that you 'ad them ideas."

He drank up his beer and went off 'ome, shaking his 'cad, and, arter three or four of'em 'ad explained to George Kettle wot he meant, George went off 'ome, too.

The week afore Christmas, Smith, the landlord, said as 'ow he 'ad got enough money, and three days arter we all came up 'ere to see the prize drawn. It was one o' the biggest hampers Smith could get; and there was a fine, large turkey in it, a large goose, three pounds o' pork sausages, a bottle o' whiskey, a bottle o' rum, a bottle o' brandy, a bottle o' gin, and two bottles o' wine. The hamper was all decorated with holly, and a little flag was stuck in the top.

On'y men as belonged was allowed to feel the turkey and the goose, and arter a time Smith said as 'ow p'r'aps they'd better leave off, and 'e put all the things back in the hamper and fastened up the lid.

"How are we going to draw the lottery?" ses John Biggs, the blacksmith.

"There'll be twenty-three bits o' paper," ses Smith, "and they'll be numbered from one to twenty-three. Then they'll be twisted up all the same shape and put in this 'ere paper bag, which I shall 'old as each man draws. The chap that draws the paper with the figger on it wins."

He tore up twenty-three bits o' paper all about the same size, and then with a black-lead pencil 'e put the numbers on, while everybody leaned over 'im to see fair play. Then he twisted every bit o' paper up and held them in his 'and.

"Is that satisfactory?" he ses.

"Couldn't be fairer," ses Bill Chambers.

"Mind," ses Smith, putting them into a tall paper bag that had 'ad sugar in it and shaking them up, "Number I wins the prize. Who's going to draw fust?"

All of 'em hung back and looked at each other; they all seemed to think they'd 'ave a better chance when there wasn't so many numbers left in the bag.

"Come on," ses Smith, the landlord. "Some-body must be fust."

"Go on, George Kettle," ses Bob Pretty. "You're sure to win. I 'ad a dream you did."

"Go on yourself," ses George.

"I never 'ave no luck," ses Bob; "but if Henery Walker will draw fust, I'll draw second. Somebody must begin."

"O' course they must," ses Henery, "and if you're so anxious why don't you 'ave fust try?"

Bob Pretty tried to laugh it off, but they wouldn't 'ave it, and at last he takes out a pocket-'andkerchief and offers it to Smith, the landlord.

"All right, I'll go fust if you'll blindfold me," he ses.

"There ain't no need for that, Bob," ses Mr. Smith. "You can't see in the bag, and even if you could it wouldn't help you."

"Never mind; you blindfold me," ses Bob; "it'll set a good example to the others."

Smith did it at last, and when Bob Pretty put his 'and in the bag and pulled out a paper you might ha' heard a pin drop.

"Open it and see what number it is, Mr. Smith," ses Bob Pretty. "Twenty-three, I expect; I never 'ave no luck."

Smith rolled out the paper, and then 'e turned pale and 'is eyes seemed to stick right out of his 'ead.

"He's won it!" he ses, in a choky voice. "It's Number I. Bob Pretty 'as won the prize."

You never 'eard such a noise in this 'ere public-'ouse afore or since; everybody shouting their 'ardest, and Bill Chambers stamping up and down the room as if he'd gone right out of his mind.

"Silence!" ses Mr. Smith, at last. "Silence! How dare you make that noise in my 'ouse, giving it a bad name? Bob Pretty 'as won it fair and square. Nothing could ha' been fairer. You ought to be ashamed o' yourselves."

Bob Pretty wouldn't believe it at fust. He said that Smith was making game of 'im, and, when Smith held the paper under 'is nose, he kept the handkerchief on his eyes and wouldn't look at it.

"I've seen you afore to-day," he says, nodding his 'ead. "I like a joke as well as anybody, but it ain't fair to try and make fun of a pore, 'ard-working man like that."

I never see a man so astonished in my life as Bob Pretty was, when 'e found out it was really true. He seemed fair 'mazed-like, and stood there scratching his 'ead, as if he didn't know where 'e was. He come round at last, arter a pint o' beer that Smith 'ad stood 'im, and then he made a little speech, thanking Smith for the fair way he 'ad acted, and took up the hamper.

"'Strewth, it is heavy," he ses, getting it up on his back. "Well, so long, mates."

"Ain't you—ain't you going to stand us a drink out o' one o' them bottles?" ses Peter Gubbins, as Bob got to the door.

Bob Pretty went out as if he didn't 'ear; then he stopped, sudden-like, and turned round and put his 'ead in at the door agin, and stood looking at 'em.

"No, mates," he ses, at last, "and I wonder at you for asking, arter what you've all said about me. I'm a pore man, but I've got my feelings. I drawed fust becos nobody else would, and all the thanks I get for it is to be called a thief."

He went off down the road, and by and by Bill Chambers, wot 'ad been sitting staring straight in front of 'im, got up and went to the door, and stood looking arter 'im like a man in a dream. None of 'em seemed to be able to believe that the lottery could be all over so soon, and Bob Pretty going off with it, and when they did make up their minds to it, it was one o' the most miserable sights you ever see. The idea that they 'ad been paying a pint a week for Bob Pretty for months nearly sent some of 'em out of their minds.

"It can't be 'elped," ses Mr. Smith. "He 'ad the pluck to draw fust, and he won; anybody else might ha' done it. He gave you the offer, George Kettle, and you, too, Henery Walker."

Henery Walker was too low-spirited to answer 'im; and arter Smith 'ad said "Hush!" to George Kettle three times, he up and put 'im outside for the sake of the 'ouse.

When 'e came back it was all quiet and everybody was staring their 'ardest at little Dicky Weed, the tailor, who was sitting with his head in his 'ands, thinking, and every now and then taking them away and looking up at the ceiling, or else leaning forward with a start and looking as if 'e saw something crawling on the wall.

"Wot's the matter with you?" ses Mr. Smith.

Dicky Weed didn't answer 'im. He shut his eyes tight and then 'e jumps up all of a sudden. "I've got it!" he says. "Where's that bag?"

"Wot bag?" ses Mr. Smith, staring at 'im. "The bag with the papers in," ses Dicky.

"Where Bob Pretty ought to be," ses Bill Chambers. "On the fire."

"Wot?" screams Dicky Weed. "Now you've been and spoilt everything!"

"Speak English," ses Bill.

"I will!" ses Dicky, trembling all over with temper. "Who asked you to put it on the fire? Who asked you to put yourself forward? I see it all now, and it's too late."

"Wot's too late?" ses Sam Tones.

"When Bob Pretty put his 'and in that bag," ses Dicky Weed, holding up 'is finger and looking at them, "he'd got a bit o' paper already in it—a bit o' paper with the figger I on it. That's 'ow he done it. While we was all watching Mr. Smith, he was getting 'is own bit o' paper ready."

He 'ad to say it three times afore they understood 'im, and then they went down on their knees and burnt their fingers picking up bits o' paper that 'ad fallen in the fireplace. They found six pieces in all, but not one with the number they was looking for on it, and then they all got up and said wot ought to be done to Bob Pretty.

"You can't do anything," ses Smith, the landlord. "You can't prove it. After all, it's only Dicky's idea."

Arf-a-dozen of 'em all began speaking at once, but Bill Chambers gave 'em the wink, and pretended to agree with 'im.

"We're going to have that hamper back," he ses, as soon as Mr. Smith 'ad gone back to the bar, "but it won't do to let 'im know. He don't like to think that Bob Pretty was one too many for 'im."

"Let's all go to Bob Pretty's and take it," ses Peter Gubbins, wot 'ad been in the Militia.

Dicky Weed shook his 'ead. "He'd 'ave the lor on us for robbery," he ses; "there's nothing he'd like better."

They talked it over till closing-time, but nobody seemed to know wot to do, and they stood outside in the bitter cold for over arf an hour still trying to make up their minds 'ow to get that hamper back. Fust one went off 'ome and then another, and at last, when there was on'y three or four of 'em left, Henery Walker, wot prided himself on 'is artfulness, 'ad an idea.

"One of us must get Bob Pretty up 'ere to-morrow night and stand 'im a pint, or p'r'aps two pints," he ses. "While he's here two other chaps must 'ave a row close by his 'ouse and pretend to fight. Mrs. Pretty and the young 'uns are sure to run out to look at it, and while they are out another chap can go in quiet-like and get the hamper."

It seemed a wunnerful good idea, and Bill Chambers said so; and 'e flattered Henery Walker up until Henery didn't know where to look, as the saying is.

"And wot's to be done with the hamper when we've got it?" ses Sam Jones.

"Have it drawed for agin," ses Henery. "It'll 'ave to be done on the quiet, o' course."

Sam Jones stood thinking for a bit. "Burn the hamper and draw lots for everything separate," 'e ses, very slow. "If Bob Pretty ses it's 'is turkey and goose and spirits, tell 'im to prove it. We sha'n't know nothing about it."

Henery Walker said it was a good plan; and arter talking it over they walked 'ome all very pleased with theirselves. They talked it over next day with the other chaps; and Henery Walker said arterwards that p'r'aps it was talked over a bit too much.

It took 'em some time to make up their minds about it, but at last it was settled that Peter Gubbins was to stand Bob Pretty the beer; Ted Brown, who was well known for his 'ot temper, and Joe Smith was to 'ave the quarrel; and Henery Walker was to slip in and steal the hamper, and 'ide the things up at his place.

Bob Pretty fell into the trap at once. He was standing at 'is gate in the dark, next day, smoking a pipe, when Peter Gubbins passed, and Peter, arter stopping and asking 'im for a light, spoke about 'is luck in getting the hamper, and told 'im he didn't bear no malice for it.

"You 'ad the pluck to draw fust," he ses, "and you won."

Bob Pretty said he was a Briton, and arter a little more talk Peter asked 'im to go and 'ave a pint with 'im to show that there was no ill-feeling. They came into this 'ere Cauliflower public-'ouse like brothers, and in less than ten minutes everybody was making as much fuss o' Bob Pretty as if 'e'd been the best man in Claybury.

"Arter all, a man can't 'elp winning a prize," ses Bill Chambers, looking round.

"I couldn't," ses Bob.

He sat down and 'elped hisself out o' Sam Jones's baccy-box; and one or two got up on the quiet and went outside to listen to wot was going on down the road. Everybody was wondering wot was happening, and when Bob Pretty got up and said 'e must be going, Bill Chambers caught 'old of him by the coat and asked 'im to have arf a pint with 'im.

Bob had the arf-pint, and arter that another one with Sam Jones, and then 'e said 'e really must be going, as his wife was expecting 'im. He pushed Bill Chambers's 'at over his eyes—a thing Bill can't abear—and arter filling 'is pipe agin from Sam Jones's box he got up and went.

"Mind you," ses Bill Chambers, looking round, "if 'e comes back and ses somebody 'as taken his hamper, nobody knows nothing about it."

"I 'ope Henery Walker 'as got it all right," ses Dicky Weed. "When shall we know?"

"He'll come up 'ere and tell us," ses Bill Chambers. "It's time 'e was here, a'most."

Five minutes arterwards the door opened and Henery Walker came staggering in. He was as white as a sheet, his 'at was knocked on one side of his 'ead, and there was two or three nasty-looking scratches on 'is cheek. He came straight to Bill Chambers's mug—wot 'ad just been filled—and emptied it, and then 'e sat down on a seat gasping for breath.

"Wots the matter, Henery?" ses Bill, staring at 'im with 'is mouth open.

Henery Walker groaned and shook his 'ead. "Didn't you get the hamper?" ses Bill, turning pale. Henery Walker shook his 'ead agin.

"Shut up!" he ses, as Bill Chambers started finding fault. "I done the best I could. Nothing could ha' 'appened better—to start with. Directly Ted Brown and Joe Smith started, Mrs. Pretty and her sister, and all the kids excepting the baby, run out, and they'd 'ardly gone afore I was inside the back door and looking for that hamper, and I'd hardly started afore I heard them coming back agin. I was at the foot o' the stairs at the time, and, not knowing wot to do, I went up 'em into Bob's bedroom."

"Well?" ses Bill Chambers, as Henery Walker stopped and looked round.

"A'most direckly arterwards I 'eard Mrs. Pretty and her sister coming upstairs," ses Henery Walker, with a shudder. "I was under the bed at the time, and afore I could say a word Mrs. Pretty gave a loud screech and scratched my face something cruel. I thought she'd gone mad."

"You've made a nice mess of it!" ses Bill Chambers.

"Mess!" ses Henery, firing up. "Wot would you ha' done?"

"I should ha' managed diff'rent," ses Bill Chambers. "Did she know who you was?"

"Know who I was?" ses Henery. "O' course she did. It's my belief that Bob knew all about it and told 'er wot to do."

"Well, you've done it now, Henery," ses Bill Chambers. "Still, that's your affair."

"Ho, is it?" ses Henery Walker. "You 'ad as much to do with it as I 'ad, excepting that you was sitting up 'ere in comfort while I was doing all the work. It's a wonder to me I got off as well as I did."

Bill Chambers sat staring at 'im and scratching his 'ead, and just then they all 'eard the voice of Bob Pretty, very distinct, outside, asking for Henery Walker. Then the door opened, and Bob Pretty, carrying his 'ead very 'igh, walked into the room.

"Where's Henery Walker?" he ses, in a loud voice.

Henery Walker put down the empty mug wot he'd been pretending to drink out of and tried to smile at 'im.

"Halloa, Bob!" he ses.

"What was you doing in my 'ouse?" ses Bob Pretty, very severe.

"I—I just looked in to see whether you was in, Bob," ses Henery.

"That's why you was found under my bed, I s'pose?" ses Bob Pretty. "I want a straight answer, Henery Walker, and I mean to 'ave it, else I'm going off to Cudford for Policeman White."

"I went there to get that hamper," ses Henery Walker, plucking up spirit. "You won it unfair last night, and we determined for to get it back. So now you know."

"I call on all of you to witness that," ses Bob, looking round. "Henery Walker went into my 'ouse to steal my hamper. He ses so, and it wasn't 'is fault he couldn't find it. I'm a pore man and I can't afford such things; I sold it this morning, a bargain, for thirty bob."

"Well, then there's no call to make a fuss over it, Bob," ses Bill Chambers.

"I sold it for thirty bob," ses Bob Pretty, "and when I went out this evening I left the money on my bedroom mantelpiece—one pound, two arf-crowns, two two-shilling pieces, and two sixpences. My wife and her sister both saw it there. That they'll swear to."

"Well, wot about it?" ses Sam Jones, staring at 'im.

"Arter my pore wife 'ad begged and prayed Henery Walker on 'er bended knees to spare 'er life and go," ses Bob Pretty, "she looked at the mantel-piece and found the money 'ad disappeared."

Henery Walker got up all white and shaking and flung 'is arms about, trying to get 'is breath.

"Do you mean to say I stole it?" he ses, at last.

"O' course I do," ses Bob Pretty. "Why, you said yourself afore these witnesses and Mr. Smith that you came to steal the hamper. Wot's the difference between stealing the hamper and the money I sold it for?"

Henery Walker tried for to answer 'im, but he couldn't speak a word.

"I left my pore wife with 'er apron over her 'ead sobbing as if her 'art would break," ses Bob Pretty; "not because o' the loss of the money so much, but to think of Henery Walker doing such a thing— and 'aving to go to jail for it."

"I never touched your money, and you know it," ses Henery Walker, finding his breath at last. I don't believe it was there. You and your wife 'ud swear anything."

"As you please, Henery," ses Bob Pretty. "Only I'm going straight off to Cudford to see Policeman White; he'll be glad of a job, I know. There's three of us to swear to it, and you was found under my bed."

"Let bygones be bygones, Bob," ses Bill Chambers, trying to smile at 'im.

"No, mate," ses Bob Pretty. "I'm going to 'ave my rights, but I don't want to be 'ard on a man I've known all my life; and if, afore I go to my bed to-night, the thirty shillings is brought to me, I won't say as I won't look over it."

He stood for a moment shaking his 'ead at them, and then, still holding it very 'igh, he turned round and walked out.

"He never left no money on the mantelpiece," ses Sam Jones, at last.

"Don't you believe it. You go to jail, Henery."

"Anything sooner than be done by Bob Pretty," ses George Kettle.

"There's not much doing now, Henery," ses Bill Chambers, in a soft voice.

Henery Walker wouldn't listen to 'em, and he jumped up and carried on like a madman. His idea was for 'em all to club together to pay the money, and to borrow it from Smith, the landlord, to go on with. They wouldn't 'ear of it at fust, but arter Smith 'ad pointed out that they might 'ave to go to jail with Henery, and said things about 'is license, they gave way. Bob Pretty was just starting off to see Policeman White when they took the money, and instead o' telling 'im wot they thought of 'im, as they 'ad intended, Henery Walker 'ad to walk alongside of 'im and beg and pray of 'im to take the money. He took it at last as a favor to Henery, and bought the hamper back with it next morning— cheap. Leastways, he said so.

THE RESURRECTION OF MR. WIGGETT

Mr. Sol Ketchmaid, landlord of the Ship, sat in his snug bar, rising occasionally from his seat by the taps to minister to the wants of the customers who shared this pleasant retreat with him.

Forty years at sea before the mast had made Mr. Ketchmaid an authority on affairs maritime; five years in command of the Ship Inn, with the nearest other licensed house five miles off, had made him an autocrat.

From his cushioned Windsor-chair he listened pompously to the conversation. Sometimes he joined in and took sides, and on these occasions it was a foregone conclusion that the side he espoused would win. No matter how reasonable the opponent's argument or how gross his personalities, Mr. Ketchmaid, in his capacity of host, had one unfailing rejoinder—the man was drunk. When Mr. Ketchmaid had pronounced that opinion the argument was at an end. A nervousness about his license—conspicuous at other times by its absence—would suddenly possess him, and, opening the little wicket which gave admission to the bar, he would order the offender in scathing terms to withdraw.

Twice recently had he found occasion to warn Mr. Ned Clark, the village shoemaker, the strength of whose head had been a boast in the village for many years. On the third occasion the indignant shoemaker was interrupted in the middle of an impassioned harangue on free speech and bundled into the road by the ostler. After this nobody was safe.

To-night Mr. Ketchmaid, meeting his eye as he entered the bar, nodded curtly. The shoemaker had stayed away three days as a protest, and the landlord was naturally indignant at such contumacy.

"Good evening, Mr. Ketchmaid," said the shoemaker, screwing up his little black eyes; "just give me a small bottle o' lemonade, if you please."

Mr. Clark's cronies laughed, and Mr. Ketchmaid, after glancing at him to make sure that he was in earnest, served him in silence.

"There's one thing about lemonade," said the shoemaker, as he sipped it gingerly; "nobody could say you was drunk, not if you drank bucketsful of it."

There was an awkward silence, broken at last by Mr. Clark smacking his lips.

"Any news since I've been away, chaps?" he inquired; "or 'ave you just been sitting round as usual listening to the extra-ordinary adventures what happened to Mr. Ketchmaid whilst a-foller-ing of the sea?"

"Truth is stranger than fiction, Ned," said Mr. Peter Smith, the tailor, reprovingly.

The shoemaker assented. "But I never thought so till I heard some o' the things Mr. Ketchmaid 'as been through," he remarked.

"Well, you know now," said the landlord, shortly.

"And the truthfullest of your yarns are the most wonderful of the lot, to my mind," said Mr. Clark.

"What do you mean by the truthfullest?" demanded the landlord, gripping the arms of his chair.

"Why, the strangest," grinned the shoemaker.

"Ah, he's been through a lot, Mr. Ketchmaid has," said the tailor.

"The truthfullest one to my mind," said the shoemaker, regarding the landlord with spiteful interest, "is that one where Henry Wiggett, the boatswain's mate, 'ad his leg bit off saving Mr. Ketchmaid from the shark, and 'is shipmate, Sam Jones, the nigger cook, was wounded saving 'im from the South Sea Highlanders."

"I never get tired o' hearing that yarn," said the affable Mr. Smith.

"I do," said Mr. Clark.

Mr. Ketchmaid looked up from his pipe and eyed him darkly; the shoemaker smiled serenely.

"Another small bottle o' lemonade, landlord," he said, slowly.

"Go and get your lemonade somewhere else," said the bursting Mr. Ketchmaid.

"I prefer to 'ave it here," rejoined the shoemaker, "and you've got to serve me, Ketchmaid. A licensed publican is compelled to serve people whether he likes to or not, else he loses of 'is license."

"Not when they're the worse for licker he ain't," said the landlord.

"Certainly not," said the shoemaker; "that's why I'm sticking to lemonade, Ketchmaid."

The indignant Mr. Ketchmaid, removing the wire from the cork, discharged the missile at the ceiling. The shoemaker took the glass from him and looked round with offensive slyness.

"Here's the 'ealth of Henry Wiggett what lost 'is leg to save Mr. Ketchmaid's life," he said, unctuously. "Also the 'ealth of Sam Jones, who let hisself be speared through the chest for the same noble purpose. Likewise the health of Captain Peters, who nursed Mr. Ketchmaid like 'is own son when he got knocked up doing the work of five men as was drowned; likewise the health o' Dick Lee, who helped Mr. Ketchmaid capture a Chinese junk full of pirates and killed the whole seventeen of 'em by—'Ow did you say you killed 'em, Ketchmaid?"

The landlord, who was busy with the taps, affected not to hear.

"Killed the whole seventeen of 'em by first telling 'em yarns till they fell asleep and then choking 'em with Henry Wiggett's wooden leg," resumed the shoemaker.

"Kee—hee," said a hapless listener, explosively. "Kee—hee—kee—"

He checked himself suddenly, and assumed an air of great solemnity as the landlord looked his way.

"You'd better go 'ome, Jem Summers," said the fuming Mr. Ketchmaid. "You're the worse for liker."

"I'm not," said Mr. Summers, stoutly.

"Out you go," said Mr. Ketchmaid, briefly. "You know my rules. I keep a respectable house, and them as can't drink in moderation are best outside."

"You should stick to lemonade, Jem," said Mr. Clark. "You can say what you like then."

Mr. Summers looked round for support, and then, seeing no pity in the landlord's eye, departed, wondering inwardly how he was to spend the remainder of the evening. The company in the bar gazed at each other soberly and exchanged whispers.

"Understand, Ned Clark," said the indignant Mr. Ketchmaid, "I don't want your money in this public-house. Take it somewhere else."

"Thank'ee, but I prefer to come here," said the shoemaker, ostentatiously sipping his lemonade. "I like to listen to your tales of the sea. In a quiet way I get a lot of amusement out of 'em."

"Do you disbelieve my word?" demanded Mr. Ketchmaid, hotly.

"Why, o' course I do," replied the shoemaker; "we all do. You'd see how silly they are yourself if you only stopped to think. You and your sharks!—no shark would want to eat you unless it was blind."

Mr. Ketchmaid allowed this gross reflection on his personal appearance to pass unnoticed, and for the first time of many evenings sat listening in torment as the shoemaker began the narration of a series of events which he claimed had happened to a seafaring nephew. Many of these bore a striking resemblance to Mr. Ketch-maid's own experiences, the only difference being that the nephew had no eye at all for the probabilities.

In this fell work Mr. Clark was ably assisted by the offended Mr. Summers. Side by side they sat and quaffed lemonade, and burlesqued the landlord's autobiography, the only consolation afforded to Mr. Ketchmaid consisting in the reflection that they were losing a harmless pleasure in good liquor. Once, and once only, they succumbed to the superior attractions of alcohol, and Mr. Ketchmaid, returning from a visit to his brewer at the large seaport of Burnsea, heard from the ostler the details of a carouse with which he had been utterly unable to cope.

The couple returned to lemonade the following night, and remained faithful to that beverage until an event transpired which rendered further self-denial a mere foolishness.

It was about a week later, Mr. Ketchmaid had just resumed his seat after serving a customer, when the attention of all present was attracted by an odd and regular tapping on the brick-paved passage outside. It stopped at the tap-room, and a murmur of voices escaped at the open door. Then the door was closed, and a loud, penetrating voice called on the name of Sol Ketchmaid.

"Good Heavens!" said the amazed landlord, half-rising from his seat and falling back again, "I ought to know that voice."

"Sol Ketchmaid," bellowed the voice again; "where are you, shipmate?"

"Hennery Wig-gett!" gasped the landlord, as a small man with ragged whiskers appeared at the wicket, "it can't be!"

The new-comer regarded him tenderly for a moment without a word, and then, kicking open the door with an unmistakable wooden leg, stumped into the bar, and grasping his outstretched hand shook it fervently.

"I met Cap'n Peters in Melbourne," said the stranger, as his friend pushed him into his own chair, and questioned him breathlessly. "He told me where you was."

"The sight o' you, Hennery Wiggett, is better to me than diamonds," said Mr. Ketchmaid, ecstatically. "How did you get here?"

"A friend of his, Cap'n Jones, of the barque Venus, gave me a passage to London," said Mr. Wiggett, "and I've tramped down from there without a penny in my pocket."

"And Sol Ketchmaid's glad to see you, sir," said Mr. Smith, who, with the rest of the company, had been looking on in a state of great admiration. "He's never tired of telling us 'ow you saved him from the shark and 'ad your leg bit off in so doing."

"I'd 'ave my other bit off for 'im, too," said Mr. Wiggett, as the landlord patted him affectionately on the shoulder and thrust a glass of spirits into his hands. "Cheerful, I would. The kindest-'earted and the bravest man that ever breathed, is old Sol Ketchmaid."

He took the landlord's hand again, and, squeezing it affectionately, looked round the comfortable bar with much approval. They began to converse in the low tones of confidence, and names which had figured in many of the landlord's stories fell continuously on the listeners' ears.

"You never 'eard anything more o' pore Sam Jones, I s'pose?" said Mr. Ketchmaid.

Mr. Wiggett put down his glass.

"I ran up agin a man in Rio Janeiro two years ago," he said, mournfully. "Pore old Sam died in 'is arms with your name upon 'is honest black lips."

"Enough to kill any man," muttered the discomfited Mr. Clark, looking round defiantly upon his murmuring friends.

"Who is this putty-faced swab, Sol?" demanded Mr. Wiggett, turning a fierce glance in the shoemaker's direction.

"He's our cobbler," said the landlord, "but you don't want to take no notice of 'im. Nobody else does. He's a man who as good as told me I'm a liar."

"Wot!" said Mr. Wiggett, rising and stumping across the bar; "take it back, mate. I've only got one leg, but nobody shall run down Sol while I can draw breath. The finest sailor-man that ever trod a deck is Sol, and the best-'earted."

"Hear, hear," said Mr. Smith; "own up as you're in the wrong, Ned."

"When I was laying in my bunk in the fo'c's'le being nursed back to life," continued Mr. Wig-gett, enthusiastically, "who was it that set by my side 'olding my 'and and telling me to live for his sake?—why, Sol Ketchmaid. Who was it that said that he'd stick to me for life?—why Sol Ketchmaid. Who was it said that so long as 'e 'ad a crust I should have first bite at it, and so long as 'e 'ad a bed I should 'ave first half of it?—why, Sol Ketchmaid!"

He paused to take breath, and a flattering murmur arose from his listeners, while the subject of his discourse looked at him as though his eloquence was in something of the nature of a surprise even to him.

"In my old age and on my beam-ends," continued Mr. Wiggett, "I remembered them words of old Sol, and I knew if I could only find 'im my troubles were over. I knew that I could creep into 'is little harbour and lay snug. I knew that what Sol said he meant. I lost my leg saving 'is life, and he is grateful."

"So he ought to be," said Mr. Clark, "and I'm proud to shake 'ands with a hero."

He gripped Mr. Wiggett's hand, and the others followed suit. The wooden-legged man wound up with Mr. Ketchmaid, and, disdaining to notice that that veracious mariner's grasp was somewhat limp, sank into his chair again, and asked for a cigar.

"Lend me the box, Sol," he said, jovially, as he took it from him. "I'm going to 'and 'em round. This is my treat, mates. Pore old Henry Wig-gett's treat."

He passed the box round, Mr. Ketchmaid watching in helpless indignation as the customers, discarding their pipes, thanked Mr. Wiggett warmly, and helped themselves to a threepenny cigar apiece. Mr. Clark was so particular that he spoilt at least two by undue pinching before he could find one to his satisfaction.

Closing time came all too soon, Mr. Wiggett, whose popularity was never for a moment in doubt, developing gifts to which his friend had never even alluded. He sang comic songs in a voice which made the glasses rattle on the shelves, asked some really clever riddles, and wound up with a conjuring trick which consisted in borrowing half a crown from Mr. Ketchmaid and making it pass into the pocket of Mr. Peter Smith. This last was perhaps not quite so satisfactory, as the utmost efforts of the tailor failed to discover the coin, and he went home under a cloud of suspicion which nearly drove him frantic.

"I 'ope you're satisfied," said Mr. Wiggett, as the landlord, having shot the bolts of the front door, returned to the bar.

"You went a bit too far," said Mr. Ketchmaid, shortly; "you should ha' been content with doing what I told you to do. And who asked you to 'and my cigars round?"

"I got a bit excited," pleaded the other.

"And you forgot to tell 'em you're going to start to-morrow to live with that niece of yours in New Zealand," added the landlord.

"So I did," said Mr. Wiggett, smiting his forehead; "so I did. I'm very sorry; I'll tell 'em tomorrow night."

"Mention it casual like, to-morrow morning," commanded Mr. Ketchmaid, "and get off in the arternoon, then I'll give you some dinner besides the five shillings as arranged."

Mr. Wiggett thanked him warmly, and, taking a candle, withdrew to the unwonted luxury of clean sheets and a soft bed. For some time he lay awake in deep thought and then, smothering a laugh with the bed-clothes, he gave a sigh of content and fell asleep.

To the landlord's great annoyance his guest went for a walk next morning and did not return until the evening, when he explained that he had walked too far for his crippled condition and was unable to get back. Much sympathy was manifested for him in the bar, but in all the conversation that ensued Mr. Ketchmaid listened in vain for any hint of his departure. Signals were of no use, Mr. Wiggett merely nodding amiably and raising his glass in response; and when, by considerable strategy, he brought the conversation from pig-killing to nieces, Mr. Wiggett deftly transferred it to uncles and discoursed on pawn-broking.

The helpless Mr. Ketchmaid suffered in silence, with his eye on the clock, and almost danced with impatience at the tardiness of his departing guests. He accompanied the last man to the door, and then, crimson with rage, returned to the bar to talk to Mr. Wiggett.

"Wot d'y'r mean by it?" he thundered.

"Mean by what, Sol?" inquired Mr. Wiggett, looking up in surprise.

"Don't you call me Sol, 'cos I won't have it," vociferated the landlord, standing over him with his fist clenched. "First thing to-morrow morning off you go."

"Off?" repeated the other in amazement. "Off? Whereto?"

"Anywhere," said the overwrought landlord; "so long as you get out of here, I don't care where you go."

Mr. Wiggett, who was smoking a cigar, the third that evening, laid it carefully on the table by his side, and regarded him with tender reproach.

"You ain't yourself, Sol," he said, with conviction; "don't say another word else you might say things you'll be sorry for."

His forebodings were more than justified, Mr. Ketchmaid indulging in a few remarks about his birth, parentage, and character which would have shocked an East-end policeman.

"First thing to-morrow morning you go," he concluded, fiercely. "I've a good mind to turn you out now. You know the arrangement I made with you."

"Arrangement!" said the mystified Mr. Wiggett; "what arrangements? Why, I ain't seen you for ten years and more. If it 'adn't been for meeting Cap'n Peters—"

He was interrupted by frenzied and incoherent exclamations from Mr. Ketchmaid.

"Sol Ketchmaid," he said, with dignity, "I 'ope you're drunk. I 'ope it's the drink and not Sol Ketchmaid, wot I saved from the shark by 'aving my leg bit off, talking. I saved your life, Sol, an' I 'ave come into your little harbour and let go my little anchor to stay there till I go aloft to join poor Sam Jones wot died with your name on 'is lips."

He sprang suddenly erect as Mr. Ketchmaid, with a loud cry, snatched up a bottle and made as though to brain him with it.

"You rascal," said the landlord, in a stifled voice. "You infernal rascal. I never set eyes on you till I saw you the other day on the quay at Burnsea, and, just for an innercent little joke like with Ned Clark, asked you to come in and pretend."

"Pretend!" repeated Mr. Wiggett, in a horror-stricken voice. "Pretend! Have you forgotten me pushing you out of the way and saying, 'Save yourself, Sol,' as the shark's jaw clashed together over my leg? Have you forgotten 'ow—?"

"Look 'ere," said Mr. Ketchmaid, thrusting an infuriated face close to his, "there never was a Henery Wiggett; there never was a shark; there never was a Sam Jones!"

"Never—was—a—Sam Jones!" said the dazed Mr. Wiggett, sinking into his chair. "Ain't you got a spark o' proper feeling left, Sol?"

He fumbled in his pocket, and producing the remains of a dirty handkerchief wiped his eyes to the memory of the faithful black.

"Look here," said Mr. Ketchmaid, putting down the bottle and regarding him intently, "you've got me fair. Now, will you go for a pound?"

"Got you?" said Mr. Wiggett, severely; "I'm ashamed of you, Sol. Go to bed and sleep off the drink, and in the morning you can take Henry Wiggett's 'and, but not before."

He took a box of matches from the bar and, relighting the stump of his cigar, contemplated Mr. Ketchmaid for some time in silence, and then, with a serious shake of his head, stumped off to bed. Mr. Ketchmaid remained below, and for at least an hour sat thinking of ways and means out of the dilemma into which his ingenuity had led him.

He went to bed with the puzzle still unsolved, and the morning yielded no solution. Mr. Wiggett appeared to have forgotten the previous night's proceedings altogether, and steadfastly declined to take umbrage at a manner which would have chilled a rhinoceros. He told several fresh anecdotes of himself and Sam Jones that evening; anecdotes which, at the immediate risk of choking, Mr. Ketchmaid was obliged to indorse.

A week passed, and Mr. Wiggett still graced with his presence the bar of the Ship. The landlord lost flesh, and began seriously to consider the advisability of making a clean breast of the whole affair. Mr. Wiggett watched him anxiously, and with a skill born of a life-long study of humanity, realised that his visit was drawing to an end. At last, one day, Mr. Ketchmaid put the matter bluntly.

"I shall tell the chaps to-night that it was a little joke on my part," he announced, with grim decision; "then I shall take you by the collar and kick you into the road."

Mr. Wiggett sighed and shook his head.

"It'll be a terrible show-up for you," he said, softly. "You'd better make it worth my while, and I'll tell 'em this evening that I'm going to New Zealand to live with a niece of mine there, and that you've paid my passage for me. I don't like telling any more lies, but, seeing it's for you, I'll do it for a couple of pounds."

"Five shillings," snarled Mr. Ketchmaid.

Mr. Wiggett smiled comfortably and shook his head. Mr. Ketchmaid raised his offer to ten shillings, to a pound, and finally, after a few remarks which prompted Mr. Wiggett to state that hard words broke no bones, flung into the bar and fetched the money.

The news of Mr. Wiggett's departure went round the village at once, the landlord himself breaking the news to the next customer, and an overflow meeting assembled that evening to bid the emigrant farewell.

The landlord noted with pleasure that business was brisk. Several gentlemen stood drink to Mr. Wiggett, and in return he put his hand in his own pocket and ordered glasses round. Mr. Ketchmaid, in a state of some uneasiness, took the order, and then Mr. Wiggett, with the air of one conferring inestimable benefits, produced a lucky halfpenny, which had once belonged to Sam Jones, and insisted upon his keeping it.

"This is my last night, mates," he said, mournfully, as he acknowledged the drinking of his health. "In many ports I've been, and many snug pubs I 'ave visited, but I never in all my days come across a nicer, kinder-'earted lot o' men than wot you are."

"Hear, hear," said Mr. Clark.

Mr. Wiggett paused, and, taking a sip from his glass to hide his emotion, resumed.

"In my lonely pilgrimage through life, crippled and 'aving to beg my bread," he said, tearfully, "I shall think o' this 'appy bar and these friendly faces. When I am wrestlin' with the pangs of 'unger and being moved on by the 'eartless police, I shall think of you as I last saw you."

"But," said Mr. Smith, voicing the general consternation, "you're going to your niece in New Zealand?"

Mr. Wiggett shook his head and smiled a sad, sweet smile.

"I 'ave no niece," he said, simply; "I'm alone in the world."

At these touching words his audience put their glasses down and stared in amaze at Mr. Ketchmaid, while that gentleman in his turn gazed at Mr. Wiggett as though he had suddenly developed horns and a tail.

"Ketchmaid told me hisself as he'd paid your passage to New Zealand," said the shoemaker; "he said as 'e'd pressed you to stay, but that you said as blood was thicker even than friendship."

"All lies," said Mr. Wiggett, sadly. "I'll stay with pleasure if he'll give the word. I'll stay even now if 'e wishes it."

He paused a moment as though to give his bewildered victim time to accept this offer, and then addressed the scandalised Mr. Clark again.

"He don't like my being 'ere," he said, in a low voice. "He grudges the little bit I eat, I s'pose. He told me I'd got to go, and that for the look o' things 'e was going to pretend I was going to New Zealand. I was too broke-'earted at the time to care wot he said—I 'ave no wish to sponge on no man—but, seeing your 'onest faces round me, I couldn't go with a lie on my lips—Sol Ketch-maid, old shipmate—good-bye."

He turned to the speechless landlord, made as though to shake hands with him, thought better of it, and then, with a wave of his hand full of chastened dignity, withdrew. His stump rang with pathetic insistence upon the brick-paved passage, paused at the door, and then, tapping on the hard road, died slowly away in the distance. Inside the Ship the shoemaker gave an ominous order for lemonade.

William Wymark Jacobs was born on September 8, 1863 in the Wapping district of London, England. An author, humorist and dramatist, Jacobs is best remembered for the enduring classic tale of horror - "The Monkey's Paw".

As a youth, Jacobs grew up near the Wapping docks in London, where his father was a wharf manager. The family's first home was home was a house on a River Thames wharf.

The docklands setting would show up frequently in his later literary output. Jacobs, the wharf rat, and his three siblings lost their mother when they were all still young children. Their father, William Gage Jacobs, remarried and fathered a further seven children with his erstwhile housekeeper Ellen Florey. Although he grew up surrounded by poverty, Jacobs himself received a formal education in London, first at a private prep school and later at the Birkbeck Literary and Scientific Institute (now part of the University of London and known as Birkbeck College).

Jacobs' adult working life began with a clerical position at the Post Office Savings Bank. The job was not a stimulating one but Jacobs put his imagination to good use and started to write short stories, sketches and articles, many of which appeared in the Post Office house publication "Blackfriars Magazine."

Although Jacobs did receive his fair share of rejection slips at the beginning of his career, many works written during this period of clerical employment appeared in the "Idler" and "Today" magazines, both of which were edited by noted humorist Jerome K. Jerome, who had taken a liking to Jacobs' stories.

From 1898, Jacobs also published stories in "The Strand", a popular, monthly fiction and general interest magazine. The arrangement stayed in place for most of his life and many of the works in Jacobs' subsequent collections – including the nautical serialization A Master of Craft (1899-1900) - appeared there first.

Jacobs' first volume of collected works was published in 1896. Many Cargoes, a selection of sea-faring yarns, established Jacobs as a popular writer and humorist with a penchant for authentic dialogue and trick endings (critics of the day referred to him as the "O. Henry of the Waterfront").

A year later he published a novelette, The Skipper's Wooing, and in 1898 and another collection of short stories titled Sea Urchins. These works painted vivid, if imaginatively stretched, pictures of dockland and seafaring London with colourful characters (such as "The Night Watchman", Ginger Dick) that now seem archetypal.

Many of Jacobs' periodical publications and first editions were illustrated with woodcuts and ink drawings, as was still the custom at the turn of the 20th century. The author worked regularly with artists such as E.W. Kemble, who had illustrated Mark Twain's Adventures of Huckleberry Finn and Harriet Beecher Stowe's Uncle Tom's Cabin, and his good friend Will Owen, who eventually became a household name on the strength of his iconic Bisto Kids, Bovril and Lux Soap advertising posters.

By 1899, Jacobs was able to quit the post office and finally begin a career making a living as a full-time writer.

He married the noted suffragist Agnes Eleanor Williams (who had been jailed for her protest activities) in 1900. They set up a household in Loughton, Essex as well as living part of the year in central London. The couple went on to have five children together though their marriage was considered an unhappy one.

The publication of two short novels: At Sunwich Port (a romantic tale of rival sea captains in the fictional seaside community of Sunwich standing in for the actual East England community of Sandwich, Kent) and Dialstone Lane (another small town romance involving intrigue and buried treasure), in 1902 and 1904 respectively, cemented Jacobs' reputation as one of the leading British authors of the new century.

On the foundations of a continuing ability to write for his audience he was readily published though he never strayed too far from what was becoming his familiar, dependable style. There followed a string of further successful publications, including Captain's All (1905), Night Watches (1914), The Castaways (1916), and Sea Whispers (1926). Jacobs published eighteen books in all during his lifetime; thirteen collections and five novels.

As a storyteller, Jacobs is perhaps better remembered for a handful of brief tales of the supernatural than for his popular nautical-themed works. The most famous of these, The Monkey's Paw, originally appeared as part of the 1902 short story collection The Lady of the Barge. It is an economically written story about a shriveled talisman, a monkey's paw that brings grief and horror in the wake of all too literal wish granting. The story has been adapted for other media repeatedly, starting with a one-act play performed at London's Haymarket Theatre in 1903. There have been multiple film adaptations of the story in the modern era; some of us are familiar with its appearance in an episode of the popular animated series, The Simpsons.

Another macabre gem, The Toll-House, was published as part of the collection Sailor's Knots in 1909. Jacob's once again employs a sparse style to tell the story of a group of men who spend the night in a famously haunted house on a dare (a noticeably similar narrative concept was put to use in the much earlier play The Ghost of Jerry Bundler, which had launched Jacobs' parallel career as a dramatist back in 1899 when it was produced at the St. James Theatre in London). Innovative at the time of writing, these sparingly written, atmospheric ghost stories are now familiar classics of the supernatural genre.

Though prolific in his younger years, Jacobs' productivity dropped dramatically after the start of World War I. Yet even in self-imposed semi-retirement Jacobs was still recognized as a leading humorist, ranked alongside such writers as P. G. Wodehouse and George Birmingham. He enjoyed continuing influence and elevated status among his fellow writers as evidenced by these comments attributed to his colleague Henry James:

"Mr. Jacobs, I envy you. You are popular! Your admirable work is appreciated by a wide circle of readers; it has achieved popularity. Mine never goes into a second edition."

James' literary fortunes would, of course, change, but his back-handedly complimentary admiration is compelling evidence of Jacobs' reputation as a writer and humourist both for his audience and his perhaps more admired literary colleagues.

Though Jacobs would create little in the way of new work after 1911, he was still writing. In these later years, seemingly burnt out creatively, Jacobs concentrated more on writing dramatizations and adaptations of his existing stories, including Beauty and the Barge (a film version starring Margaret Rutherford was also released in 1937) and In the Dark (a one act play that is often performed pr published with The Monkey's Paw adaptation).

Though admired by loyal readers throughout his lifetime, Jacobs has been almost completely forgotten since. Critics are at a loss to name a single reason why - Jacobs is universally considered to be a fine and imaginative literary craftsman. But, as critic John Wain suggested in a 1960 essay, perhaps Jacobs' humour may have been too gentle to persist into the cruel and sarcastic modern era, his dry pokes at proletariat hardship no longer suiting the times.

Nonetheless, Jacobs' legacy remains solid: he continued Dickens' (a writer with whom he is also often compared) tradition for sharing working class stories in authentic vernacular. And polished narratives such as The Monkey's Paw set a standard for the clever use of horror in fiction and popular culture that endures to this day. Indeed recently his works have begun to show an increased demand and appreciation in a world that is constantly looking over its shoulder.

William Wymark Jacobs died in a North London nursing home in Hornsey Lane, Islington on September 1st, 1943, just a week before his 80th birthday.

W.W. Jacobs – A Concise Bibliography

NOVELS AND SHORT STORY COLLECTIONS
MANY CARGOES (SHORT STORIES) (1896)
THE SKIPPER'S WOOING (1897)
SEA URCHINS (SHORT STORIES) (1898) aka MORE CARGOES
A MASTER OF CRAFT (1900)
LIGHT FREIGHTS (SHORT STORIES) (1901)
THE LADY OF THE BARGE (SHORT STORIES) (1902)
AT SUNWICH PORT (1902)
DIALSTONE LANE (1902)
SALTHAVEN (1908)
CAPTAINS ALL (SHORT STORIES) (1911)
NIGHT WATCHERS (SHORT STORIES) (1914)
DEEP WATERS (SHORT STORIES) (1919)

SHORT STORIES (INCLUDING THOSE USED IN THE COLLECTIONS ABOVE)
A BENEFIT PERFORMANCE
A BLACK AFFAIR
A CASE OF DESERTION
A CHANGE OF TREATMENT
A CIRCULAR TOUR
A DISCIPLINARIAN
A DISTANT RELATIVE
A GARDEN PLOT
A GOLDEN VENTURE
A HARBOUR OF REFUGE
A LOVE KNOT
A LOVE PASSAGE
A MARKED MAN
A MIXED PROPOSAL
A RASH EXPERIMENT
A SAFETY MATCH

A SPIRIT OF AVARICE
A TIGER'S SKIN
ADMIRAL PETERS
AFTER THE INQUEST
ALF'S DREAM
AN ADULTERATION ACT
AN ELABORATE ELOPEMENT
AN INTERVENTION
AN ODD FREAK
ANGELS' VISITS
BACK TO BACK
BEDRIDDEN
THE WINTER OFFENSIVE
THE BEQUEST
BILL'S LAPSE
BILL'S PAPER CHASE
BLUNDELL'S IMPROVEMENT
THE BOATSWAIN'S WATCH
THE BOATSWAIN'S MATE
BOB'S REDEMPTION
BREAKING A SPELL
BREVET RANK
BROTHER HUTCHINS
THE BULLY OF THE "CAVENDISH"
THE CABIN PASSENGER
CAPTAIN ROGERS
THE CAPTAIN'S EXPLOIT
CAPTAINS ALL
THE CASTAWAY
THE CHANGELING
"CHOICE SPIRITS"
THE CONSTABLE'S MOVE
CONTRABAND OF WAR
THE CONVERT
THE COOK OF THE "GANNET"
CUPBOARD LOVE
DESERTED
DIRTY WORK
THE DISBURSEMENT SHEET
DIXON'S RETURN
DOUBLE DEALING
THE DREAMER
DUAL CONTROL
EASY MONEY
ESTABLISHING RELATIONS
FAIRY GOLD
FALSE COLOURS
FAMILY CARES
FINE FEATHERS
FOR BETTER OR WORSE
THE FOUR PIGEONS

FRIENDS IN NEED
GOOD INTENTIONS
THE GREY PARROT
THE GUARDIAN ANGEL
THE HEAD OF THE FAMILY
HER UNCLE
HIS LORDSHIP
HIS OTHER SELF
HOMEWARD BOUND
HUSBANDRY
IN BORROWED PLUMES
IN LIMEHOUSE REACH
IN MID-ATLANTIC
IN THE FAMILY
IN THE LIBRARY
JERRY BUNDLER
KEEPING UP APPEARANCES
KEEPING WATCH
THE LADY OF THE BARGE
LAWYER QUINCE
THE LOST SHIP
LOW WATER
MADE TO MEASURE
THE MADNESS OF MR. LISTER
"MANNERS MAKYTH MAN"
MATED
"MATRIMONIAL OPENINGS"
MIXED RELATIONS
MONEY CHANGERS
THE MONEY-BOX
THE MONKEY'S PAW
MRS. BUNKER'S CHAPERON
THE NEST EGG
ODD MAN OUT
THE OLD MAN OF THE SEA
OUTSAILED
OVER THE SIDE
PAYING OFF
THE PERSECUTION OF BOB PRETTY
PETER'S PENCE
PICKLED HERRING
PRIVATE CLOTHES
PRIZE MONEY
THE RESURRECTION OF MR. WIGGETT
THE RIVAL BEAUTIES
RULE OF THREE
SAM'S BOY
SAM'S GHOST
SELF-HELP
SENTENCE DEFERRED
SHAREHOLDERS

SKILLED ASSISTANCE
THE SKIPPER OF THE "OSPREY"
SMOKED SKIPPER
STEPPING BACKWARDS
STRIKING HARD
THE SUBSTITUTE
THE TEMPTATION OF SAMUEL BURGE
THE TEST
THE THREE SISTERS
TO HAVE AND TO HOLD
"THE TOLL-HOUSE"
TWIN SPIRITS
TWO OF A TRADE
THE UNDERSTUDY
THE UNKNOWN
THE VIGIL
WATCH-DOGS
THE WEAKER VESSEL
THE WELL
THE WHITE CAT

STAGE
THE GHOST OF JERRY BUNDLER (1899) (In London)

FILM ADAPTATIONS
A MASTER OF CRAFT (1922)
THE MONKEY'S PAW (1933)
OUR RELATIONS, a Laurel & Hardy film, "suggested by" to Jacobs' "The Money Box." (1936)
FOOTSTEPS IN THE FOG, from the short story The Interruption. (1955)